W9-CAN-961

EDGAR'S WORST SUNDAY

sands press
Brockville, Ontario

EDGAR'S WORST SUNDAY

BRAD OATES

sands press

sands press

A Division of 10361976 Canada Inc.
300 Central Avenue West
Brockville, Ontario
K6V 5V2

Toll Free 1-800-563-0911 or 613-345-2687
http://www.sandspress.com

ISBN 978-1-988281-53-7
Copyright © 2018 Brad Oates
http://www.BradOHInc.com
All Rights Reserved

Cover Design by Kristine Barker and Wendy Treverton
Edited by Alyssa Owen
Formatting by Renee Hare
Publisher Kristine Barker

For information on bulk purchases of this book or any book published by Sands Press, please call 1-800-563-0911.

1st Printing October 2018

To book an author for your live event, please call: 1-800-563-0911

Sands Press is a literary publisher interested in new and established authors wishing to develop and market their product. For more information please visit our website at www.sandspress.com.

CHAPTER 1
THE PEARLY GATE

For as long as he could remember, Sunday mornings for Edgar Vincent had been a painful haze of sickness and regret. On many such mornings, he'd awoken, and pressing shaky forefingers against pounding temples to steady his vision, watched the world assemble itself into appalling mockeries of intentions he barely remembered having the night before.

From the delicate and well-rehearsed act of lightly removing a dainty arm draped over him in its peaceful slumber, to gathering his scattered belongings from amid the less-valued refuse of storm drains, Edgar had long since grown accustomed to Sunday's special brand of cruelty.

Some had been spent poring over unending lists of indecipherable text messages and records of inappropriate outgoing calls as his brain turned over in the dry interior of his skull—planning an increasingly complex series of explanations and excuses.

Other Sundays had found him shielding his eyes as he stumbled down the radiant aisles of his local drugstore. Every time he ended up there, it seemed harder to locate the essential combination of cover-ups to conceal the scars of his failed endeavours.

Once, he'd woken up comfortably in bed, only to find he had sorely tested the patience of its rightful owner the night before while explaining how certain he was that it was, in fact, his own. That morning had been a hasty retreat—frustrated especially when every attempted apology he offered was rudely rebuffed by his unwilling host, who only repeated that he'd already heard enough bullshit from Edgar to last a lifetime.

Edgar's friends liked to relate one story about an especially obscene Sunday morning involving his disturbing abuse of a freshly stolen "Slip-n-Slide." He had no recollection of this incident, however, and had long since settled on its falseness.

Still, none of that would ever compare to the day Edgar died.

An ongoing source of frustration for him—in part because it had always

1

acted as the herald to his greatest regrets—was the first ray of sun which crept surreptitiously through his blinds each Sunday morning, waking him from his dead sleep and calling him back into the realm of the accountable.

Today, it was far worse. Even as the sun rose upon the scene of his demise, a glaring light penetrated Edgar's eyelids, searing into them and charring his very being. "Fuck off!" he rolled over, but it was no good.

His lashes cracked apart painfully as he slowly forced his eyes open to take in his surroundings and begin to decipher the sentence of this particular Sabbath. He had little enough to start with—his memory was a taint of flashing lights, loud voices, and the lingering uncertainty that had always played the harbinger to his poor decisions.

Glancing about, Edgar searched for the usual suspects but found them sorely lacking. Where he instinctually expected dirty alleys and broken bottles, he found only pristine white, as if he'd somehow awoken in an unsullied arctic tundra—which would be a first even for him.

Dragging a rough hand across his face and burrowing the heels of his palms into each eye, in turn, he slowly pushed himself up to one side as the pain in his head sloshed about like the ice-diluted remains in a discarded highball glass.

"Fucking hell," he mumbled, his deep voice breaking the otherwise perfect silence as he steadied himself, trying to wrestle up any certain account of the previous night's decisions. "Bad," he speculated, "they were definitely very bad."

Few memories came—an indistinct image of a distant building, tall and ominous, yet its recollection filled Edgar with an unusual longing. Beyond that were only vague flashes of bars and lights, bits of laughter and the thrill of alcohol passing over lips. These swirled about in their regular pantomime, sliding slowly in and out of the familiar haze which always preceded his blackouts. There was little more, just the building far off in front of him, and a strange feeling of imbalance. Imbalance, then fear—terrible, paralyzing fear.

After that, his memories faded into nothing but a strange, calm sense of understanding. In the end, he was still left with no guess as to his present whereabouts.

Mustering his strength, Edgar inhaled deeply. The air was sweet, like half-remembered childhood nature-walks. All was still and peaceful, and the temperature seemed to perfectly match his own; a comforting bath embracing his tired body. He struggled to his feet.

Everything was white. White—and very bright. Wherever he looked,

Edgar was blinded by a brilliant light. Squinting against its intrusion and grinding his dry lips, he found that his mouth tasted like stale cigarettes and whiskey. *Only one flavour short of the Trinity*, he noted.

"Where am I?" he wondered aloud as he forced himself into motion—with such a homogenous environment, one direction seemed as good as any other. His only certainty was that he was ready to move on from wherever he was. "So much damn white!"

Straining his eyes against the unearthly glare, he managed to discern a vast outline in the distance, and continued on, feeling somewhat encouraged.

His hands were weak and clumsy as he reached down to straighten out his jeans—which he was surprised to find splendidly clean. Swallowing down a sudden lump in his throat, Edgar slowed his pace and passed his hands carefully over his body, instinctually falling into his familiar Sunday morning check: keys, wallet, phone, shoes, hair, teeth—all there. Better than he could have hoped.

With his sense of relief growing, he lifted a hand up to his eyes to fend off the glare and determined to get on with his day.

The titanic object ahead was much closer already, far too close for the short time he'd been walking. It now encompassed the entirety of his vision: tall, impenetrable, and—golden.

What the...

Edgar took a hesitant step forward, then another. The obstruction grew clearer with each trembling step, until with a splitting headache and gaping jaw, he found himself staring at an endless golden wall extending beyond sight in both directions.

With ornate spires stretching upward before disappearing into the white like a plane losing itself in the clouds, the wall stood as the undeniable centrepiece of his strange morning. Behind him, reality seemed to drop away into a disconcerting fog of light, and he shuddered at the thought of turning back now, feeling as if to do so would be to lose himself forever.

It took only a few more steps for Edgar to reach the structure, where he found a gate—the only one visible along the entire stretch—waiting directly in front of him. For all the pomp and flair of the wall, the entryway was a simple latticework of gold and pearl, forming two double doors of standard size. Both stood wide open.

A tall man waited directly beside the gate with serene patience. Edgar hadn't noticed him until that very moment and was caught quite off-guard. The stranger's silvery hair was cropped short, and his casual white clothing blended perfectly with the luminous haze surrounding them. He eyed Edgar with a knowing expression.

Tensing, Edgar tried to shake off the mixed sense of dread and guilt which crept through him under the man's pacified gaze. Only after an uncomfortably long wait did he accept that he would need to be the one to break the silence.

"Am I in…"

The man smiled, an old and understanding gesture, but only continued to watch Edgar reassuringly through piercing grey eyes.

"…heaven?" he finished, with only the faint hint of a blush appearing on his smooth-shaven cheeks.

"If you like." The man's voice was deep, yet not old. It was strong, but timeless—the creaking of a great oak in a passing storm.

"So, I'm dead?" Edgar pushed, swearing a solemn oath that his friends would pay dearly if this proved to be some elaborate ruse.

"Yes."

"And this is the afterlife?"

"It is as you say."

Rolling his dark brown eyes, Edgar suddenly realized the shortcoming of his previous effort at taking inventory. Reaching back once more, he was relieved to find his cigarettes in their customary place. The pack was full as he flipped the lid open and drew one out, which seemed odd after a night of what he could only surmise to be prodigious drinking.

"Heaven. Jesus Christ!" Flicking his lighter to life, he took a long drag.

The man maintained his composure despite Edgar's blasphemy. No uncomfortable grimace, no hasty, embarrassed self-blessing. Not even a damned ironic chuckle. Something was very wrong; Edgar never failed to get a rise out of those who thought they knew better.

"So then, Pete, is it?" Edgar waited briefly for a response, but finding himself disappointed, continued. "I suppose you're meant to read from my life-book? Tally my sins; decide if I can enter…all that?"

"The door is open to you."

Stoic bastard, thought Edgar. "Now that's just lazy. I'm pretty sure it's your entire purpose to recount the story of my life, and frankly, that stands to be the most enjoyable part of this whole debacle."

"You know your story better than I, Mr. Vincent."

The smoke rushed from Edgar's nostrils like the trail of a falling airliner, dancing about the strange man's face. "Don't call me that."

"As you say," the man replied, offering an apologetic nod.

"If this is really heaven, why the hell am I getting in? Priests have actually told me I'm going to hell…more than once! Do you even have a list? Cause I've got to say, man, your standards seem pretty damn low."

"My standards are not the issue," the man answered, his tone never fluctuating.

"Oh, fuck you!" Edgar was irate now. Debauchery, he cherished. Disrespect, he could stomach. Even open ridicule could be endured. "You call this heaven? Clouds and golden gates? Humourless old men with no relevant answers? This isn't heaven, it's just…it's fucking…cliché!" he spat the last word like he'd just drunk deeply from his own snakebite.

The man did not respond, his only answer a sympathetic smile.

Edgar finished his cigarette with one last pull and flicked the butt down into the fog at the man's feet, where it died with a serpentine hiss. He finally decided—much to his chagrin—that he would be forced to relent. "Ok, I'll cooperate. What am I meant to do?"

"You've already done all you were ever meant to, Edgar. The rest is up to you."

Such starry-eyed sincerity always left Edgar with an urge to spike the drink of whatever naive nitwit had the gall to hold onto such childish delusions. Rolling his eyes again, trying to be more noticeable this time, he reached back and grabbed his cigarette pack. Opening it, he glanced down to find it still full. "Oh God…"

"No," the man chimed in, and Edgar was certain he detected a flicker of amusement behind his calm repose.

"Well…" Edgar acquiesced, remembering a time-tested truth—when the realities of Sunday were too harsh, a strategic retreat back to Saturday was only a few bottles away. "Does heaven at least have a bar?"

"If you wish." The man nodded and extended a long arm to gesture gracefully through the gate.

"Well, that's a start," Edgar admitted. "If you'll excuse me, Petey, I've got a toast to make to a beautiful son-of-a-bitch who died before his time." With that, he passed heedlessly under the intricate pearl inlay of the gate and walked with only a mild stagger off into the bright nothing beyond.

5

CHAPTER 2
THE LOCAL BAR

The former life of Edgar Vincent had never been rife with ritual. In fact, he made every effort imaginable—and some beyond imagining—to avoid it whenever possible. Still, some level of routine did slip in, and he couldn't keep vigil forever. And so, by the time he met his demise at the age of 32, there existed a small collection of routines that he had come not only to rely upon, but to fully endorse.

Primary among these, and holding the special distinction of being the only thing Edgar would commit to calling sacred, was his customary celebration of a job well done. As a moderately respected independent film composer, these moments were not uncommon, but he reserved this particular celebration for only the most monumental of accomplishments. On such occasions, he would put on the first—and only—tie he'd ever owned in his adult life, sit down in his big old office chair, then crack open the most expensive bottle of scotch he had.

The scotch—purchased only just before a score's completion as an anticipatory measure—would be consumed as he sat in contemplative silence, listening to the completed work with a broad smile painted across his devilishly handsome face.

Inevitably, this ritual would lead him out the door once the scotch and music were finished—Edgar possessed an uncanny skill for synchronizing these events—and off into countless adventures which he would never fully recall.

Further to the list of ingrained habits, Edgar was certain to call his dear friend Emeric at the earliest possible convenience each time he bedded a new woman. Emeric, never being fond of this particular ritual, had over the years begun to answer Edgar's calls with less and less reliability, but Edgar remained unconvinced of any correlation, attributing it rather to Emeric's apparent lack of courtesy.

Edgar would also call his mother on each major Christian holiday, and even did his best to conceal the pain in his voice when she inevitably harangued him with the meaning of the day, and what lessons he might take from it.

Most truly ingrained habits aside from these were minor and were only noted by those who knew him well—who in truth were rather few and far between. He took a shot before sitting down in every bar he visited. He often drank high-end cocktails, but made a point to always request at least one small, subtle change. He avoided public washrooms whenever possible, although history—and police records—indicated he had absolutely no qualms about actual public urination.

However, among the various quirks and rituals Edgar had permitted over the course of his life, one of his most cherished had been his bi-weekly Saturday nights out with his inner circle of friends during university. This of course should not be taken to imply that drinking only once every two weeks had ever been the standard for Edgar—quite the contrary—but rather that even in the wild days of his youth, he had still been certain to put that small slot of time aside to meet with some of his most valued comrades, and partake in some of his most enjoyed activities.

A goddamn drink would be nice, he mused woefully. With each step, the soft white glow puffed up around his feet like billowing clouds, and he wandered blindly through the haze, his footsteps coming like old memories.

His head still swam, the inside of his skull scraping like sandpaper. From somewhere in his uncertain surroundings, Edgar thought he could hear a soft, delicate voice singing. *Seems about right*, he acknowledged, *can't have clouds and golden gates without some harp-brandishing asshole singers.*

How did I end up in this hellhole? Racking his tired brain for answers, he came up dreadfully short—still, logic could get him far enough.

Whenever Edgar woke up feeling this bad, he could be certain that at least one of the usual suspects were involved. *Could this be Duncan's fault?* he asked himself.

It was a distinct possibility, given the length of their friendship and shared passion for excess. But it had been a long while since Duncan and Edgar really tied one on, and in truth, he'd long suspected that Duncan was slowing down.

Again, his thoughts turned to days long past, and the endless shenanigans he and his friends had engaged in back at their old crawl, The Scholar's Lament. It had started with just Duncan and himself, having grown up together, but it certainly increased from there.

There's no way Emeric would have let things get this out of control, Edgar surmised.

Emeric had joined the group some way into their first year of university, and while he'd never matched the unchecked hedonism of either Duncan or Edgar, he did bring a certain unspoken balance to the group.

Admittedly, he did pitifully little to stop me that time with the police horse... No, he was certain that Emeric would have done something to prevent him from... *How the hell did this happen anyway?*

Continuing onward, he struggled to shake the strange sense of déjà-vu that haunted each step, and although he could see nothing but the white fog everywhere around him, his feet moved as if they knew the way, and he was far too dizzy to argue.

Duncan is too serious now, and Emeric is too responsible. Edgar raced through a mental process of elimination. The list of suspects was dwindling, and as he worked to swallow down a liberty-minded bit of bile, he shook his head dismally and hedged his bets on the culprit. *Fucking Jake,* he concluded.

The youngest member of Edgar's inner circle by two years, Jake had joined the group late, and only through sheer tenacity had he managed to be accepted at all. Still, he was dependable, and Edgar knew that beyond anyone else in his life, he could always rely on Jake when he wanted to get truly, righteously shit-canned.

It was precisely due to this ease of access that Edgar accurately considered himself quite the authority on the heinous Sunday mornings after a night out with Jake. All the tell-tale signs were there; the swimming head, the raspy throat, and the overwhelming senses of loss, confusion, and regret. Still, even as the evidence mounted, something at the back of his weary mind struggled against the tightening noose of logic, and he could not wholly commit himself to this explanation just yet.

Pulling another cigarette from his still-full pack, he trudged onward as he drew the lighter up to his mouth. With a flick of his thumb, the flame ignited, sending a soothing wave of nicotine coursing down his desert-dry throat.

If Edgar had thought he'd heard angels singing before, there was no doubt now. With a final step, the haze of fog peeled back to reveal a stout brown building with dirty windows and a flickering, neon sign: The Scholar's Lament.

The chill which ran down his spine was accompanied by a long sigh, and despite his ongoing misgivings, Edgar could imagine nowhere else he'd rather be at the moment. The place had served as a sanctuary during his 'academic career', and it was in this very bar that he'd cemented most of the defining relationships of his life.

"Another round over here!" Stepping into the large, dim room, Edgar was immediately put at ease by a familiar voice. Gazing around, he found everything in place—exactly as he remembered. The unused popcorn machine in the corner, the sprawling bookshelves full of battered hardcover tomes beautifully bound with patterns utterly unrevealing of their contents… even the tiny shelf high up in the far corner holding an odd, miniature brass motorcycle.

Tinny, outdated music played quietly from beaten up speakers mounted above the long bar, and in the far left corner opposite the door was the ugly old ceramic statue of a student toiling over an invisible project, his forehead balanced on his palm in a show of deep frustration. The intricately painted statue, as always, was covered with countless years of intimate personalized graffiti.

"Hurry up!" Once again, the voice was Duncan's, who sat beside the scholar and stared over at Edgar with an impatient smirk.

The call made Emeric turn, adjust his glasses, and send out that big, dumb smile he seemed to reserve only for the company of his friends.

"Hey Edgar," he called softly, his voice barely making its way over. Edgar moved slowly, passing strangers as his mind raced with possibilities. *How much did I drink last night?*

Draped around the shoulder of the poor busy scholar was the long, muscular arm of Jake. *How long has it been since we've all been together?* Edgar wondered as he made his way methodically through the familiar bar. *A year at least, maybe more?*

Time was cruel to young men and naïve promises, and although the four of them remained relatively close, it was an especially rare occurrence these days that their schedules allowed all of them to get together at once.

Not all, Edgar corrected himself, *not anymore.*

The three familiar faces watching him from across the room burdened Edgar once again with the nagging suspicion that perhaps his entire situation was still, somehow, the tail end of the most elaborate joke ever pulled.

A splitting hangover, a walk through an inscrutable void, and a trail of doubt leading through a golden gate and ending at his old university hangout. Doubting his sense of reality was nothing new to Edgar, but existential questioning certainly was. *How does one know if he's truly dead?* He wondered. The question was too heavy to hold in the tissue paper folds of his throbbing brain, and he let it spill out with no significant contemplation. If he was to unravel the mystery of the night before, the three men in front of him were the place to start. *Those bastards.*

If it was a cruel joke, he was certain he could rule Emeric out. The mousy little man, although clever, would never have the spine to play a trick on anyone, and Edgar least of all.

Jake certainly would have done it, but alone the drunken buffoon was about as practical as tits on a bull, and his ability to plan was even less functional. The ever-increasing complexity of the joke—if indeed it was one—meant Jake could not have done it by himself at any rate.

If anyone could have pulled this off, it would be Duncan. In his prime, Duncan was the perfect foil to Edgar—returning every joke, answering every shot, and one-upping him with every misdeed. But Duncan was Edgar's oldest friend and closest rival...if he'd done it, the crowd he assembled to witness the humiliating punch-line would have been far more significant.

Stopping in front of the table, his friends turned cheerfully to greet him. Emeric pushed his glasses up the bridge of his nose, smiled, and nodded in eager anticipation of Edgar's acknowledgment. *Definitely not Emeric...but he'll be the first one to come clean if he does know anything.*

Jake, his arm still cast about the ceramic student in a careless gesture betraying no affection, stared not at Edgar, but rather at the five shots presently being laid out by a waitress. *An exceptionally sexy waitress,* Edgar noted with restrained glee.

Duncan, meanwhile, was a picture of poise—sitting squarely against the backrest of his chair with his hands folded politely in front of him. He gave one stiff, formal nod as he spoke, "Edgar."

No one moved...no one said a word. Emeric, Edgar realized with unease, failed to pass his shot up to him, as was customary. The bar waited in purgatorial silence until a jarring sound brought Edgar's head around to the right, where a chair at the end of their table had been pulled out with a long, grating screech. Falling into it with a graceless but refreshingly characteristic plop, was Alex.

That was it for Edgar. His breath left him like a freight train making up for lost time, and he stood stuttering meekly. He had known only Duncan longer than Alex, having met the latter in his first year of university. Together, the three of them had partied and grown; they'd learned life lessons, and shared things that were...unsharable.

Everything changed after university, however. As Edgar applied himself to music and worked his way into an industry that was every bit as nepotistic and elitist as he'd imagined, Duncan had lied, stolen, and even studied his way into the ranks of a prestigious law firm. Emeric had taken up a professorship at the very university they'd all studied at, and Jake, never having chosen a major, dropped out once his friends finished their tenures, but managed to finance his nights out with Edgar by taking up construction.

Meanwhile, Alex began to drift. An inspired painter and lover of wine, women, and whimsy, Alex shared just about every characteristic of Edgar's save for the latter's respectable preference for hard liquor; that and his drive for success. While every bit as talented, even Edgar would admit that— albeit only to himself—Alex was interested only in the moment. He'd simply travelled about, never applying himself to any long-term goals.

The thing that really bothered Edgar however—and never more than this moment—was what Alex did when he'd finally come back to reunite with his old friends years later. It wasn't that they'd ever lost touch, social media made that almost impossible, it was just that they had so much proper catching up to do. So, when Alex ended up wrapping his jalopy around a tree after their first night out drinking and being carried away on a covered stretcher, it had put almost as much of a damper on the festivities as his sitting down at the table just now.

"Fuck," said Edgar. Emeric smiled up at him, his pale hand extending a shot.

"Time to get drinking boy!" bellowed Jake, as he waved, and half-spilled, a shot under the nose of the eponymous lamenting scholar.

Duncan smiled with quiet repose.

"Good to see you, buddy." Alex looked up with unabashed sincerity— he'd never lost that shit-eating clarity usually reserved for children and lunatics.

"But you're…"

The words stuck in Edgar's throat, but his table seemed to care little for the immediate completion of clauses. Instead they followed Duncan's example, and watched with good-natured patience.

"…dead," Edgar finally finished.

"Yeah," Alex agreed, shrugging his shoulders as if to indicate that it was every bit the bummer Edgar seemed to imply.

"And so am I." He needed no conductor to follow this train to its destination.

"Yeah!" Jake hollered with the drunken enthusiasm of a freshman at a strip club.

Emeric shook his head. Then, realizing the obfuscating nature of his gesture, nodded to Edgar in an exaggerated arc, blushed, and stared back down at the table.

"Afraid so, my friend," Duncan chimed in, his calm voice chiding, "you really fucked up this time."

"Thanks," Edgar mumbled.

"Now don't mope about it. It'll happen to us all eventually." While sincere communication was nearly a foreign language to Duncan, he did mean well on occasion.

"Happened to that asshole long ago," Jake declared, thrusting a meaty hand towards Alex, and spilling the majority of his shot in the process.

Alex offered only a comical shrug and an exaggerated pout. "Sorry about him," consoled Emeric.

"Let's move on from all this unpleasantness, Mr. Vincent. Here we are after all, together again!" said Duncan.

"Don't call me that!" Edgar snapped.

"Sorry Eds, didn't mean to ruin your afterlife." The self-assured smile on Duncan's face had been custom-designed long ago to raise Edgar's ire. It worked without fail.

"Drink, you losers!" Jake hoisted his near-empty shot glass into the air.

"The man is crass, but he isn't wrong," Duncan admitted, holding up his shot in turn.

With a gentle clink and a uniform motion, the five reunited friends tossed the liquor down their throats. Jake scowled darkly into his empty shot glass—seeming to suspect it of withholding—as Edgar took the chair beside Emeric. His attention lingered briefly on a final empty seat near the wall beside him, an unbidden question playing through his mind before being forced out by another.

"Holy shit!" The consideration only struck him that very moment. "Are you guys all dead too? What the hell happened to us?"

"Afraid not, mon frère, you're on this journey alone." While he enjoyed toying with Edgar, Duncan's intentions were beyond dispute. He could always be counted on to tell Edgar what he really needed to hear, and—to Edgar's endless frustration—to remind him of things he would sooner forget.

"He is." Jake's finger shot across the table again, sloppily jabbing Alex in the eye and eliciting a yelp.

"Watch it, dude! I'm dead, that doesn't mean I don't feel." Alex rubbed his eye as Jake nodded proudly.

"If you're not dead, how are you here?" Edgar demanded. "And how did both Alex and I make it to heaven for fuck's sake?"

"Maybe this is actually hell." Jake leaned forward as he spoke, placing his palms flat on the table as his eyes turned to saucers.

"Oh wow," Alex said with a chuckle, but no one at the table was willing to bite onto Jake's attempted epiphany.

Edgar grimaced over at Jake, who only lowered his eyes in an ill-fitting display of humility. "Now that that's out of the way, can we focus on the guy who just fucking died for a second? Explain to me how you guys are here."

Gulping uncouthly from his wine, Alex leaned over and placed a small hand on Edgar's forearm, "What would heaven be without friends, buddy?"

"You, I can understand, but what about the living ones?"

"Alex might not be wrong." The tips of Emeric's forefingers circled his temples as he spoke, and were soon lost in the coarse red wire of his hair. "It wouldn't be very heavenly if you had to sit around just waiting for everyone else to die."

With a sudden motion, Jake's hand flashed over in a wide arc and knocked the glasses from Emeric's face with a loud crack. "This isn't all about you Emmy, you selfish prick."

Emeric stuttered self-consciously before reaching down to gather up his glasses. Jake searched the faces of his peers for affirmation of his good deed.

"That was thoughtless, Emeric," Duncan agreed, the sarcasm in his voice readily apparent to everyone but its intended target. Jake beamed.

Edgar watched Duncan take a long sip from a glass of caramel coloured liquid—brandy—Edgar knew. *At least one of my friends has class.*

"I'm glad you shitheads are here," Edgar admitted, "…and for this bar. Heaven isn't half as bad as I'd have guessed, especially when I saw those ungodly obnoxious gates out there."

"No doubt about it. I can hardly imagine how all those Christians can stand it," said Duncan. This sent a gale of laughter around the table.

"I don't suppose their heaven would be like this at all." Emeric was dedicated to the quandary now, and seldom allowed himself to fall into the languid humour which Duncan and Edgar both loved so much.

"What is eschewed on Earth is denied beyond it… If I'd known that I would've been far less abstaining," said Edgar.

"And here twice as soon," came Duncan's quick retort.

"How did I die anyway?" he wondered aloud. "Do any of you remember anything?"

He was met with blank stares.

"What can I get for you, handsome?" The voice came from beside him, and turning, Edgar saw a stunningly beautiful server leaning in to take his order. Not the same one as before, it struck him that this one might be even more unnervingly lovely. Heaven, he decided right then, would suit him well.

"Scotch," he answered with a well-practiced smile. "Your very best," he finished, after briefly considering the occasion's special significance.

"Of course, sir." The woman curtsied deeply before she turned; a trite gesture, but sufficient at least to allow Edgar a better view of heaven than he'd had up to that point.

Finishing his wine and glancing over his shoulder to ascertain the whereabouts of his next drink, Alex returned Edgar's attention to more practical matters. "Can I bum a smoke from you?"

"Come on man, you don't even have your own smokes in heaven?" Edgar rolled his eyes but reached into his back pocket without any true resentment. Removing two from the pack, he handed one to his needy friend and lit the other for himself.

"I'm just going to go ahead and assume I can smoke in here."

"Heaven ain't so different after all," Jake declared with a guffaw.

"I just ran out," Alex grumbled defensively.

"I don't run out anymore," shared Edgar with a delighted smile. "It's like a fresh pack every time I open it up here."

"Well, you are in heaven," Emeric spoke softly, the better to dull the redundancy of his input.

"And yet my friends remain beggars?" Edgar laughed aloud.

"You are the company you keep." Jake smiled broadly, then poured the remainder of his beer down his gaping maw.

"I believe you're thinking of 'what you eat.'" Duncan spoke in an incredulous monotone.

"But I'm not even hungry." Jake was confused.

"Jesus guys…I'm beginning to dislike heaven again. Is it like this for you too, Alex?" Edgar asked.

Alex twirled his empty wine-glass absently between two thin fingers. Finally catching his attention, Edgar was answered only by an uncertain gaze.

Emeric glanced about inquisitively, eagerly soaking up every clue he could as the waitress brought out Edgar's drink.

"You're as useless in heaven as you were on Earth, Alex." Edgar spoke from the side of his mouth, skillfully managing to simultaneously sip at his scotch and take another drag from his cigarette. "This is fucking perfect. I'm dead, and I'll never even know how I died."

"Hey, I'm sure it'll come back to you eventually." Emeric set a comforting hand on Edgar's arm.

"You know what the real kicker is? I was just about done writing the score for BHI!"

Duncan turned his attention to the bar as Emeric nodded sympathetically. Alex stared vacantly into his empty glass, while Jake drifted off—his lips wrestling with some unspoken debate. This continued as Edgar drank in silence. After some time, Jake's struggle overpowered the apathy of his friends and brought them all around to gape at him in dumbfounded awe as he continued opening and closing his mouth in exaggerated movements.

Ultimately, it was Duncan who broke the silence, "BHI—it's an acronym you fucking idiot, stop trying to sound it out."

"Basic Human Indecency. Don't you remember the documentary Edgar was scoring?" Emeric always sought to play the peacemaker.

"Watch it, Emmy," Jake threatened. Edgar slumped down into his seat—his forehead finding a comfortable perch in the palm of his hand.

The table was quiet a moment, as each man considered what Edgar might need. "Don't be so glum, my pitiful pupil." Duncan reached over and gave Edgar a loving punch on the shoulder, then held up five fingers to the waitress behind the bar.

Looking up at the statue across from him, Edgar managed an ironic laugh. "Sorry guys, it's just a bit much, you know. BHI was going to be my masterwork. I was finally going to show those fuckers exactly why I'm the best. What my music would have done for that script—it was really poised to make an impact. The entire project will probably fall through now. Heaven—shit!"

Edgar lit himself another cigarette, intuitively passing one to Alex before being asked. No one spoke as the server brought out the requested round, placing them before each man in turn—scotch, beer, brandy, wine, rum and coke.

"How can a group as incompetent as all of you be here with me, if you're also still alive?" The question straddled the line between simple rhetoric and pleading sincerity with painful uncertainty as Edgar finished his first scotch and moved on to the next.

Duncan only smiled. It was not a demeaning gesture, nor even mocking. He just smiled over at his friend and allowed a moment to pass.

Edgar looked to Emeric, who nodded reassuringly. He was seldom much help, but ever the most eager in the attempt.

Alex, as always, stared off in esoteric repose. "I imagine somewhere down there, people are gathered around your body. How can you be there, and here as well?"

"Wait…" Jake leaned in, the furrow of his brow revealing the enormous exertion of his thoughts. "Am I dead, too?"

Edgar had to laugh. It was hard not to love the dumb bastard. Jake was loud, obnoxious, and stupid as a brick. Yet of all Edgar's friends, he was the most unflinchingly loyal. Like a giant dog with a mild learning disorder, his unabashed consistency had always been a great comfort to Edgar. "No," he answered his friend, "I'm sure you're just fine."

"That might be going a bit far," Alex interjected.

"You'll get it all figured out soon, Eds." Duncan rarely committed any statement to a single, candid meaning, and it was always a profound surprise to Edgar when he did. "And whatever happened for you to end up here, I'm sure it was sufficiently heinous to make us all proud of you."

"Even more than the night with the Slip-n-Slide!" Alex spoke from deep within his wine-cup, his satisfaction with the reference evident in its giddy delivery. This sent another gale of hearty laughter around the table—even Edgar took part, despite a long eye-roll and fervent shake of his head.

"Thanks," Edgar replied to Duncan after the laughter subsided. His voice came in a scratching rasp. "It's all such a blur. I know it was Saturday night, and that I was drinking. I have a few brief patches of memory, more like feelings really…I remember being very unsure, then a sudden epiphany washing over me.

"What really puzzles me though is how I ended up in heaven with you guys. What could I have possibly done to merit an afterlife of friends and booze?"

"That's a good question." Duncan smiled as he spoke. "For you to make it to heaven, your final seconds must have been monumentally heroic." Despite their shared penchant for what more refined men might consider depraved situations, Duncan looked at Edgar as a brother, and would never speak ill of him in earnest.

"What could I have possibly done, though?" Edgar mused. "Could I have sacrificed myself for someone? That sure doesn't sound like me. But still, heaven... Something doesn't add up."

"You didn't go to heaven." Jake finished his beer with a mighty swig and hammered his empty mug down on the table. "You're dead and that's it, moron. Now you're just living out your own fantasies—easy as that, you dumb motherfucker."

Emeric was visibly aghast.

Alex giggled with what he hoped would pass for nervousness.

Duncan arched his thick eyebrows and attempted to conceal the keen curl working up the sides of his mouth.

The idiot has it right, Edgar knew.

"You die, and the first thing you do is come see us..." Jake trailed off breathlessly, slowly doubling over the table as he rattled the cups with his braying laughter. "I knew it," he managed, before losing himself entirely.

In the bottom of Edgar's glass, only a mouthful of scotch remained. Between his fingertips, the orange ember of his cigarette slowly approached the filter, and sitting about him were his closest friends and confidantes. They watched him in silence—Emeric with his nervous squirming, Alex with his detached stare, and Jake gazing obliviously around for recognition of his insight. Duncan simply waited with a faint smile, a sparkle in his eye betraying the excitement with which he anticipated Edgar's response.

"Thanks, guys, I needed this." Edgar smiled, finishing the last of his scotch while snuffing his smoke out on the tabletop, leaving a long black streak.

"So, what are you going to do now? You must have a lot to process." Emeric sipped slowly from his rum and coke as he waited for an answer.

Edgar's attention wandered about the room, slowly tracing its way over the curves of the servers. "Well," he offered with a smirk, "if this place really holds anything I can dream up, I fear my time with you guys is done for now. I've seen the Golden Gate already, so that's one tourist trap down. Now, I believe I'll go see about some angels."

Emeric shook his head as a gleeful giggle burst from Alex's lips. Duncan nodded his knowing acceptance, while Jake continued laughing boisterously to himself. "Anything he could dream of—and he ends up at a table with four dudes..."

Edgar rose with conviction, a broad smile splitting his face across the centre. Turning, he crossed the floor of the bar with a swagger and passed through the heavy wooden door into the brilliant white glare outside. It wrapped around him like a blanket—a disorienting haze that was at once vivid and vague.

It made no difference; Edgar knew exactly where he was going.

CHAPTER 3
THE GOLDEN BALLROOM

Throughout his brief tenure in the realm of the living, Edgar had valued one thing above all others—himself. It had never been much of a competition, really.

This isn't to say that Edgar failed to appreciate the other exquisite pleasures in life. Indeed, there could be no disputing that he had been a passionate man. As a matter of fact, many bartenders over the years had described his passion with great admiration, speaking of his deep appreciation for their craft in the same breath with which they stressed the importance of higher education for their children.

Edgar's love of his own career was obvious, and his resulting success did much to fuel the pursuit of his more intimate affections. Bastard, cad, asshole and creep—he had been called them all. There were even women out there who might accuse him of taking for granted the gifts he'd been given, but they would be unequivocally incorrect. Edgar valued everything he had, and everything he was, for without them, he would not have been him.

He'd been asked once if he cared at all for the feelings of others, but this had struck Edgar as entirely unfair. His response, however, which in turn made liberal use of the terms "feeling" and "others," did little to further his cause.

And yet, if asked in the right way, by the right sort of girl, Edgar might have described himself simply, sincerely, as a man who longed to connect. Perhaps over a savoury meal or a film which could inspire hours of profound conversation—this to Edgar was the draw. In more intimate times, he liked to tell those deserving ladies that he found music integral to "setting the mood." And yet, he would inevitably finish, he never did complain about a girl who liked to perform a cappella.

It wasn't that he was a mean-spirited man, or that he was ever eager to hurt those around him—it was, according to Edgar, merely that he was willing to work harder and push further for what he wanted.

And what a man wants is often what defines him.

The white haze fell away from Edgar as he moved with the predatory gait of a prowling panther. High walls towered up around him, illuminated by multi-coloured flashes coming from all angles. He wore his old leather jacket—a friend that had gone along with him more faithfully than many he'd called his friends throughout his all-too-short life. It was simple brown leather, entirely barren of metal studs or unnecessary flaps; Edgar was a class act after-all, not some try-hard biker.

Aside from the jacket's reliable comfort and devilishly suave appearance, it had one quality which Edgar valued above any other—the uncanny effect of bringing to others the intrinsic joy that he felt should be the natural result of his company.

Perhaps it was not everyone who took this joy from the jacket. Indeed, it was entirely possible the effect was one conjured primarily in his own imagination, but there was no doubt it did wonders to complement his already dangerously charming look. This, in turn, served to secure it as the perfect companion when Edgar set out to indulge in the other two great loves of his life.

I'll start with a light cocktail, he decided. Sliding up to a bar on his left as he scouted for an opportune perch to hunt for his third and final love, he was driven nearly mad by the titillating selection he saw on offer.

She caught his eye from the far end of the bar, drawing him towards her with telekinetic surety. Edgar didn't know the woman but was instantly eager to correct that glaring error. As he crossed the long, dim chamber, however, it was neither the perfection of her curves nor the abundance of tantalizingly exposed flesh that really struck him.

Her eyes were drops of onyx in rust, calling out to him from behind their lustrous sheen. Her face was long and mocha-coloured, and the scarlet of her lips was teased by the shiny flicker of her tongue passing from one side to the other as she stared through Edgar, anticipating his approach.

Only just shorter than Edgar, she stood all curves and edges. Pointed nails played against powerful thighs draped in blue silk. Legs sleek and shiny as if they were forged of bronze stretched up from dainty feet in black heels—then up some more.

Delicate arms hung carelessly down from her exposed shoulders—slick as melting ice. Their gentle angles cascaded down with the serenity of a hidden waterfall tumbling into a lost valley, and Edgar wanted only to take the plunge over that sheer precipice.

She was just the sort of sight that would on any other day have caught

Edgar's attention in a heartbeat and imprisoned it for, well, a night at least. Nevertheless, however deserving she may have been, she was not what stood out to him as he slid up to her with the practiced swagger of a well-aged rock star.

To his right, he noticed another beauty staring with equal intensity. If she was any less stunning, Edgar couldn't say. Behind her, a large cluster of ladies exuded the same ethereal beauty. Each existed in a state of breath-taking perfection, their physical dissimilarities never taking from one or adding to another, but working rather in perfect conjunction to create a smorgasbord of delectably lascivious options. "I think I'm in…" Edgar caught himself just in time to avoid stating the obvious.

"You look like you could use a shot." The voice of the woman in blue was a breath of fire passing over him, bringing his blood to an instant boil. She stepped towards him as she spoke, holding two tall shots of clear liquor just below the captivating glow of her smile.

"You sure know how to make a man feel welcome." Edgar beamed. His voice was deep and smooth, its tones flowing into one another with the same well-rehearsed elegance as the grin he wore.

"I'm Jasmine; it's a pleasure to meet you."

"Edgar Vincent." He gave a single, firm nod of his head as he spoke. "But the night is still young, and the pleasure just began."

"You're so funny!" Jasmine replied in a gale of gentle laughter, and from all around the sound was taken up, like the slow-rising clamour of bells announcing the coming of dawn.

Taking the shot held out for him, Edgar chuckled to himself. *It's a funny thing,* he reflected, *how one great love begets another.* His head still spun from the drinks at The Scholar, yet despite the painful throbbing of his pulse booming through his temples, he couldn't help but marvel at the precision with which all of his desires were materializing about him.

All things considered, it should hardly come as a surprise, he reminded himself, raising the shot into the air as Jasmine did likewise. With a self-satisfied sigh, Edgar looked up at the shot glass, appreciating the way it bent and refracted the crisscrossing beams of light, creating a dizzying display. He had everything he could want—gorgeous women, fine booze, and the one thing truly necessary to make all the others worthwhile.

"To me!" Edgar declared, and Jasmine met his glass with a gentle clink.

"To you!" she happily attested, tossing her hair about as she poured the liquor neatly down her throat.

With a devilish grin, Edgar threw his own head back, and felt the familiar pull of his jacket's soft leather against his neck. He put the drink away with authority, focusing on the fire as it eased its way down his throat, alighting upon the tinder in his stomach and setting his soul ablaze.

The sound of the empty glass slamming down on the bar was lost in the sudden swell of music filling the room; the bass buffeting Edgar's body like the wrath of a cuckolded husband. Sweeping his head around in a broad arc, he opened his eyes and let the remaining alcohol fumes flare out from his nostrils.

Flashing lights bounced about the room like spirits chasing each other through the ether, and whenever they found cause to linger a moment, illuminating some hidden crevice, Edgar was inevitably thrilled with the treasures thus revealed.

Like the Valkyrie themselves the angels swooped down upon him, and the enormous hall was filled with the sounds of their excited chatter. In all the colours of the rainbow—and several colours left out of it entirely—they pressed towards him. There were women tall and short, athletic and petite. He saw women with skin as pale as porcelain and others as dark as the night. Some had that doe-eyed innocence which Edgar had always found so endearing, while others stared at him through eyes burning with undisguised carnality.

Never one to miss an opportunity, Edgar's mind raced with the proactive calculation of a miser determined to spend his fortune lest he finally suffocate beneath it. "Let's take this party somewhere a bit more comfortable," he called to no angel in particular, and not waiting for any specific response, set off across the busy hall.

The walls—distant in every direction he looked—were tall to the point of being ludicrous, and shone with such a radiance of gold that Edgar was left only to conclude this was not the work of some overly sensational paint-job, but rather the extravagant construction of a mind unable to perceive the hyperbolic nature of its own desires.

Edgar bit his lip.

For as far as he could see the room was packed to just short of crowded. He could, if he wished, still manage to move from one end of it to the other without overt obstruction, although the journey might be hindered either by exhaustion—as the expanse was extraordinary—or by distraction—as the temptations along the way followed in perfect suit.

The centre of the room was dominated by a fountain. Conceived entirely from a single block of solid white marble, the statue above it was of a man standing tall and proud, his broad shoulders thrown back as he stared brazenly out over the room like a captain at his prow. The man's hair was thick and well-kept, tossed playfully backward and just to the side, allowing a perfect view of his long, aquiline face.

The figure wore what appeared to be jeans, and Edgar noticed the cigarette-pack bulge in the back pocket with a grin, the drink in the large white hand with a smirk, and the intricately carved details of the leather jacket with what may have passed as the unsavory offspring of the two.

Pulling himself away from this strange sight, Edgar continued to take in his surroundings. The bar, a dark and flawless redwood, extended the entire length of one end, and it did not escape his attention to detail that its open spaces alternated perfectly with lackadaisically poised women—each skillfully advertising her own special brand of "fucking gorgeous."

Paintings were hung sparingly upon the walls, although Edgar could not bring himself to focus on their finer details. The end opposite the bar was a series of large, plush couches and loveseats, most with only a single spot left open amidst their grapevine offering of angels. As he granted his attention to each, in turn, he was enthralled to observe the reactions his gaze spawned in them. A curl of the lips here, a bat of the eye there; a flick of the tongue… Some were so blatant as to put even Edgar off—almost.

I'd need an eternity to get through this place, he mused, *even if I only had Emeric's stamina.*

Jasmine trotted happily along at his right side, barely seeming to care as Edgar cast his gaze out over the sea of sexy that seemed to be the bar's exclusive populace. Turning his sights towards an empty ring of seats in the far corner, he marched onward, and with each step, the air of the room thickened about him. Familiar rock beats slammed against and echoed off the walls, and from every angle, the throng of angels following in his stead pressed ever closer.

"Hi, I'm Tiffany!" The speaker appeared directly to his left, her hands interlaced in front of her with elbows turned outward as she bounced in place with boundless excitement. She wore a yellow dress with tiny white polka-dots, and her short blonde hair was pulled into tight symmetrical ponytails that stood out from each side of her head.

Tiffany wasted no time, and before Edgar could manage a response, she had placed a drink in his hand, and a hand on his shoulder.

All for the better, he acknowledged. Edgar had really never been one for pickup lines anyway, believing rather, that good old-fashioned sincerity was the surest way to a woman's heart. Taking in the scene with a keen eye, Edgar knew that if he could make it to these girls' hearts, he could make it anywhere he wanted…and while conventional they were not, there was an undeniable sincerity to the desires he had for the women around him.

Raising the drink to his lips, he was thrilled to find it was, in fact, an old fashioned; minus, of course, the obnoxious muddled orange enjoyed by less fashionable men.

"Well, hello Tiff…" Edgar had no opportunity to finish his sentence. Another hand grasped onto him—this one somewhat lower than his shoulder—forcing his attention immediately around to the right and freezing his procession of angels in place.

The hand clutching his manhood was thin and pale, with long red fingernails. A wave of relief flooded over Edgar as he followed the arm up, deducing that its intentions were in no way malicious as the hand moved upon him with a gentle, intentional rhythm.

The woman attached to the arm stared right through Edgar, a devious smile on her lips and a wicked challenge buried within her deep green eyes. "I'm Tyra." Her words were velvet soaked in vermouth—smooth and intoxicating.

The movements of her hand continued, causing in Edgar a stirring all his own. He raised his glass to his lips and poured graciously through their less-than-subtle curve. "It is…" he started, and watched as the wide eyes of the angels rose to meet his in a united display of eager anticipation. Being no amateur, Edgar knew better than to satisfy this desperation on demand. *Always best to let such passions stew,* he mused, his gaze drifting over the girls around him.

Jasmine stood in calm repose, burrowing into him with her dark eyes. Tiffany vibrated in place, pulling like a vacuum on the thin straw extending from her tall glass as she watched him vacantly. Tyra, still holding gently onto the increasingly tight spot in Edgar's jeans, steadied her face inches from his own, the turn of her mouth and flicker of her eyes less suggestive than explanatory. "It is indeed," she purred.

"Dessert comes later, my dear." Edgar brushed her hand gently away, certain to let his touch linger long enough to leave no doubt as to the earnestness of his implication.

Reaching back, he pulled out his packet of cigarettes, quickly sparking one to life and inhaling deeply. As the flame died away and the refreshing nicotine coursed into his bloodstream, he noticed in the halo that remained a brilliant flash of light.

It passed through the crowd just ahead of him, appearing and disappearing as it wove its way briskly through the hall. The light flickered and bounced, and it was only after a moment's concentration that Edgar perceived it to be the reflection of a dress.

The dress, as he caught a quick glimpse of it slipping through a clearing to his right, was long and silver, but that is not what caught Edgar's attention. In fact, he couldn't say what, exactly, had captivated him as he searched fruitlessly now to relocate the vision.

Inexplicably drawn, Edgar shoved through the busy room in servile fascination. Behind him came the bustle of angels, dutifully following in his hurried footsteps.

But it was gone just as suddenly as it had appeared, and among the sea of beautiful women, he could find no trace of the silver lady. With a long drag from his cigarette, he forced the fixation from his mind.

"Shall we sit?" he asked, motioning towards a ring of plush couches nestled into the corner of the room. In their midst was a small table bearing a single candle in its centre.

"Yes, let's!" Tyra's fingers clawed at his arm, pulling him towards the couch. Soon the others were following suit, pulling and prodding at him from all directions. The group moved like one unwieldy being—reckless and heedless as it made its slow, tumbling way towards the seats amidst a clamour of giggles and squeaks.

Jasmine chided, Tiffany cajoled, unknown angels forced, shoved, and directed, while Tyra's hands showed up, ever to provide the most unexpected of encouragements. Finally, the entire mass of angels—and Edgar—tumbled playfully backward, nearly spilling his drink in the process. He landed—not, he guessed, as a matter of random chance—lying prostrate upon Tyra, who let out a feline howl of faux-surprise as she stretched her neck out and pushed her chest forward.

"You know," he whispered to her, taking care to ensure his voice carried to the rest, "if I'd been told heaven was like this, I might not have avoided it as long as I did. I honestly feel a bit misled at this point."

"You poor dear!" cried Tiffany, her big, watery eyes trembling with overwhelming sympathy. Edgar laughed despite himself.

As the cluster of angels sat up and repositioned themselves amid many fumbles and squeals, Edgar stood. With a quick outward thrust of his arms, he shifted his unzipped jacket upon his shoulders. Then he tugged the collar against the back of his neck, allowing it to slide down and reposition more comfortably. It was a gesture he'd mastered over the years and one that afforded him more than comfort alone; he used the time to quickly glance about the ring of seats, taking in the lay of the land in order to determine the ideal spot for himself.

The candle flickered on the low table in the centre, which was bordered on two sides by plush red couches covered with fat velvet cushions. *Who the fuck needs so many damn pillows,* he wondered. Edgar had never been passionate about the intricacies of interior decoration.

These two were joined by a third couch, this one long and curving, which stretched around the table on the side opposite to where Edgar now stood. It was upon this couch that Tyra lay sprawled on her stomach, the scarlet of her dress nearly disappearing into the tangle of pillows cradling her as she kicked her feet about playfully.

Edgar allowed himself an ironic chuckle as he watched her take the cherry from her drink and place it—stem and all—into her mouth. *And I believe I've found my spot,* he concluded.

Jasmine and Tiffany found seats facing one another on the opposing couches, each surrounded by several angels Edgar had yet to meet. Jasmine sat with a straight back, sipping slowly from her martini glass. Across from her, Tiffany found herself in a conundrum.

Edgar watched as the energetic girl tipped her head back to drink from a fresh bottle of blue...whatever. Each time she did, however, one ponytail or the other would bump against the shoulder of her neighbour, sending her turning around to see who was touching her hair. Tiffany appeared quite flummoxed, and Edgar decided with a grin that the situation would not soon resolve itself.

Beside Tiffany, and very much aware of her neighbour's sorry plight, sat a godly huntress carved of shining obsidian. Her long, lithe body was draped loosely in an elegant white dress striped with orange. She wore her hair cropped short and tight, and showed Edgar a stunning smile as she tilted her head to the side subtly, motioning behind him.

Turning, he was surprised to find a vacant leather chair sitting upon exquisitely carved wooden legs. Edgar slid it quickly over, positioning it snugly in front of the table as he turned to face his new friend on the edge of the couch to his right. *Tyra will wait; a man simply cannot pass up a shot like this,* Edgar assured himself.

"Did someone say shots?" asked a shrill voice from behind him.

In fact, no one had, but Edgar was more than willing to disregard this insignificant oversight and cut to the delectable point. He turned to meet the speaker and found himself looking, instead, into the intoxicating sight of a freshly loaded tray of drinks.

"Cheers mutha-fuckas!" The speaker was short and thin, moving about with the searing energy of a white star as she balanced the tray with one hand and distributed drinks with the other. Edgar accepted another old fashioned with a smile, wrestling to recall the intentions he was certain he'd had just a moment before.

"That's Leslie," Jasmine spoke softly into his left ear, indicating the fast-moving girl with the tray even as she scooped up another martini for herself. Leslie toiled in a disorienting blur of frenetic grace as she made her rounds, passing out drinks with unrestrained enthusiasm.

When she'd finished with the drinks—taking the liberty, in the end, to hand everyone a tall shot of white rum—she took a seat on the couch beside Jasmine. Leslie was the shortest of the angels; a compact girl with artificially green eyes that matched her cocktail dress. Her luxurious black hair was kept shoulder length, cradling her face and complimenting her soft Asian features.

Then, as if responding to some unseen cue, the angels rose in a synchronized movement, held their shot glasses high, and with voices that flowed together like distinct parts of a greater whole, raised a toast, "Welcome to the Golden Ballroom!"

Never being one to reject a sincere toast, nor even an insincere one so long as it was properly accompanied, Edgar tossed the rum down his throat, and in a characteristic show of reckless abandonment, sent his empty shot glass sailing off into the hall behind him.

The act was mirrored instantly by the angels standing at his table, each beaming as they gazed at him anxiously. "Now that's the spirit!" Edgar spoke with glib charm, lighting yet another cigarette and pressing a finger gingerly to his temple, trying to measure how close his buzz had come to cleansing him of his raging hangover. *Not close enough,* he decided—*especially in company like this.*

Watching the angels take their seats, each staring at him with an expectant smile, Edgar decided that if any further connection was to be made, the onus of conversation would be on him. "Well," he began with a chuckle, "at least this time I won't have to clean up the broken glass."

Edgar allowed a moment to pass, looking momentarily at each of the angels as he waited for one to take the bait. When sufficient time had passed to convince him that his hope was unfounded, he determined with a sigh to soldier on.

"The last time I saw shot glasses tossed like that was actually at a party in my own office." He paused a moment longer, half curious as to whether the girls would follow his lead, while the other half—or perhaps somewhat more than that—was merely preoccupied with his old fashioned.

When he was fully satisfied on both accounts, he continued. "You know, I work scoring independent films, and it's a job that comes with certain… benefits. Anyway, I had just signed up for a major project and was trying to get started on it, albeit futilely, I'll admit.

"See, every time I really got into the zone, I found myself interrupted by unsolicited phone-calls from friends of mine. Lady-friends mostly, it's true. You see, the women in my life tend to share one thing in common—excellent taste."

This did elicit a long series of frantic giggles from the group, and Tyra licked her lips while sitting up to indiscreetly re-cross her legs in Edgar's direction.

I'll find more insight at the bottom of one of these shot glasses than I'm likely to find from any of these girls, Edgar lamented to himself, sparing a quick second to test his theory.

Coming up empty, he continued, "So, long story short, drinks were had and glasses were thrown. There may ultimately have been a stolen fire-ladder as well, but that's still a matter of speculation."

"Oh, my gosh." Tiffany blurted, sending a thin line of blue drink dribbling down her chin. "However did you get everyone out in time?"

Edgar's eyes narrowed to slits as the music continued to thud through the hall—never quite loud enough to overbear the plodding course of conversation, yet never so quiet as to allow the rhythm to escape. Staring into the flickering candle, he watched as a wisp of white smoke started its long journey from the wick up to the ceiling so very high above.

The scent reached Edgar's nostrils and stuck in his throat. *Smells like a goddamn church in here,* he thought.

Tossing down yet another shot from the tray and lighting another cigarette to help drown out the candle scent, he sank back into the firm leather of his seat. *Fucking heaven and a man still can't find a bit of compelling conversation.*

But Edgar was no stranger to stagnant small-talk, nor was he new to trying to awaken interest in strange women at bars.

"Did I mention to you girls that I'm just finishing up a…" He paused here for effect, watching the eyes of each girl widen in anticipation, "big film project? And," he continued, not allowing their obvious excitement to detract from the importance of his point, "I'm in the mood to celebrate."

This was too much for the eager crowd, which erupted immediately into an uproarious round of cheers and squeals. Tiffany jumped up and down, clapping with the vigour of a baby bird just booted from the nest.

"Yeah," he went on, sensing he was on the right track, "It's called BHI, and it's about…"

"Those things within us all—seldom spoken of, yet lingering ever just below waking consciousness." The dark woman to his right was speaking now, leaning over as her lustrous eyes burrowed into Edgar.

This sudden turn brought him around with a start. It was a rare treat indeed to meet someone with any genuine knowledge of his work. "You've heard of…"

"Basic Human Indecency?" the woman interrupted him again, "I know all about it, although perhaps, less than some."

This brought a snide chuckle and corroborative shrug from Tyra. "I simply adore your work, Edgar Vincent," the ebony angel finished.

"A woman of impeccable taste, I'm charmed. I don't believe we've met formally, although you certainly seem to know me."

"Chanel." She spoke softly and wrapped one of her long hands about his in a gentle shake as he slid towards her. "It is rare," she continued, her words slow and eloquent, "for a composer to show such distinctive acumen in his projects, likewise for a soundtrack to add so pervasively to the ambiance of a film."

Blushing, Edgar brought his glass up to his lips, but was disappointed to find it empty. "You seem impressively familiar with my accomplishments, Chanel." He fidgeted as he spoke, turning his glass around in nervous circles. Flattery was no foreign thing to Edgar and, as he sat in the extravagant trappings of The Golden Ballroom, Edgar certainly felt flattered. Chanel awaited his direction quietly; a beautiful wealth of knowledge seemingly dedicated entirely to his own passions. Around him the rest of the angels sat watching and smiling intently as they matched him drink for drink—an achievement that had sent many seasoned bar flies tumbling in the past.

Taking another drink for himself (a scotch this time, to his great delight) from the seemingly endless supply on the table before him, he found himself suddenly fixating on Jake's earlier words. This was certainly a bad sign, as any time in the past Edgar had given thought to the wisdom of his most excessive friend, it inevitably ended—poorly.

Nonetheless, no matter the quantity of liquor he consumed or the volume of the music in the grand hall—which at times dipped to barely audible when Edgar found himself engaged in conversation, and at others rose up to seize his entire being when he was bored—he could not stop Jake's voice from ringing continually through his brain. "You didn't make it to heaven," he'd said, but as Edgar looked at the shining hair of Jasmine, the mindless grin of Tiffany, and the intent focus of Chanel, the official status of this heaven seemed to be of little consequence.

Still… "You're dead and that's it, moron. Now you're just living out your own fantasy—easy as that, you dumb motherfucker." This bit sat on Edgar's conscience with greater weight.

Jesus, Jake's such an asshole, he thought.

When Jake said that, it was to the Golden Ballroom that Edgar had elected to go. Looking at it now, his stomach felt light. Turning towards the candle, Edgar watched the smoke dance and drift. Beyond it, Tyra rolled about playfully, never allowing her lustful eyes to stray from Edgar as she flicked a knotted cherry stem back and forth between her lips.

"Tell me," Chanel spoke at his side, "what really drives you?"

Edgar felt a yawn tugging at his throat. *If these girls are just the product of my own fantasy, all this flattery is really little more than spiritual masturbation.*

Edgar had certainly never been a spiritual man, avoiding the subject almost entirely ever since being old enough to dodge his grandmother's constant pleas for him to attend church with her. He was, however, an excessively proud man, and adamantly opposed to the idea of doing for himself what others could do for him.

With a lazy stretch, he pulled out his packet of cigarettes, replacing the dying one in his mouth as he stared at the sole empty space from which he'd just drawn the fresh one.

"You know," Edgar was aware of the slight slur in his speech now, but to be frank, he truly didn't give a shit, "every time I pull this pack out, I find it full. No matter how many I've already had."

"Are you," Tiffany spoke quietly, fighting to contain a shocked gasp, "magical?" Her wet eyes trembled, from fear or awe Edgar could not be bothered to guess.

"I guess everything's just turning up Edgar lately." Jasmine's voice was silk, her words still perfectly annunciated.

"Still in charge after this many drinks? You are my kinda guy!" Leslie leaned haphazardly to her left, looking like a parody of Jasmine's perfect posture to her right.

Well, he reflected, *I suppose vapid tripe still trumps opportunistic begging.* Edgar knew just what sort of reaction the observation about his smokes would have drawn from Alex.

The scotch flowed rather quickly and was followed in turn by several just like it. Tiffany bounced and cheered him along with everything he did, as Jasmine offered formal encouragement and coy agreement on his every minuscule observation.

"You are brilliant," Chanel assured him, and her hand found its way to his arm. Across the table, Tyra had managed to get an entire bushel of cherries into her mouth. Edgar could not say for certain whether her frantic choking motions were legitimate, or just the next step in her increasingly suggestive displays. Nor did he care.

All around him, the angels continued to gather—now coming; now going. It occurred to Edgar that the demographics of the crowd were continually shifting just ahead of his conscious expectations, a constant blur of fulfilled fantasies and temptations dancing before him like desert mirages.

He drew deeply from his smoke, holding it in and feeling the soothing nicotine swirl in his lungs. He tried to shake the morosity gripping him, but with every sight and sound, he could perceive the depressing pantomime of his own true desires made real.

Like a little girl crying into her journal. What kind of fucking heaven is this? he wondered. But his own thoughts betrayed him, and Edgar knew exactly who was to blame.

Another scotch, another smoke, and Edgar sank further into his seat.

Leslie stood up with a rush. As if from nowhere, she produced another tray loaded beyond belief with drinks and crisscrossed with long, powdery white lines. Edgar giddily helped himself.

Like a child choking on the dessert he'd wailed for, he wrestled with the strange sights about him. But with every attempt to banish them, the scene only grew stranger, and the heavy bass of the hall seemed poised to pound him into submission. His head rolled, his neck impotent in its function, and the lights of the hall played into one another like paint bleeding across a canvas. With a desperate surge, he straightened up in his chair and focused his vision.

If they're my creations, they can serve my fucking needs. This scene has gone entirely awry. This isn't what I need, Edgar determined, striving with his mind for mastery over his thoughts.

But Tyra was undressing now, and Chanel was passionately humming one of his finest tunes to the other angels. They swayed back and forth in intense appreciation and perfect synchronization—save for Tiffany, who continually managed to slam her pigtailed skull into the heads of the angels beside her.

"What kind of asshole dies at 32 anyway?" Edgar asked the ether.

"It's not about how old Edgar, it's about who you've been. And you, my friend, have been much too many."

With a roll of his eyes, Edgar dismissed Chanel's demented rambling, bending over instead to make another long line disappear from Leslie's silver tray.

"Dead and gone now, just another miserable fuck-up in a long line of shitheads. If I'd just made it one more year, and finished BHI, I'd have at least cemented my legacy. That would have been enough." He lit yet another smoke.

"And what is the legacy you'd have left?" Jasmine asked. Her demeanour remained a model of composure, despite having followed Edgar's example in consuming more liquor than the crew of a mid-sized fishing trawler.

"I don't even know how I died," Edgar pushed on, flatly rejecting Jasmine's bid for connection. "Now I get to sit here with you sorry lushes, with no damn clue what became of me down there. Is it down? Can anyone tell me what fucking happened?"

"The past is not my forte." It was Tyra's turn to offer solace. "But I do have a—present—here for you, and I can definitely tell you what is going to happen in the future." Her voice was confident, betraying no doubts about her assessment.

"Thanks for the offer," Edgar was interrupted by a sudden fit of hiccups, "but that's not the sort of comfort I need. I just want to know what's happened to the people I knew, where they are. Living in your head is one hell of a lonely kinda heaven!"

"You don't have to be alone," Tiffany assured him, pouting like a child with an injured bird.

"You don't know what you're talking about," Edgar dismissed the woman out of hand. "I'm alone now. Was I alone when I died, can someone at least tell me that?"

There was no answer.

Across the hall, something caught his eye. A flash of silver; there, then gone.

Edgar sighed, desperate to release the sudden wave of negativity that had taken him. Another visit to the tray helped, though not completely. "I'm sorry, it's a lot to handle you know—dying and all that. It's definitely not what I expected, but I don't blame you, I promise. Of all the angels I've ever heard of, you are by far my favourites." This resulted in a series of ahhs and gentle coos from the angels.

"I don't know exactly what I wanted from heaven. I guess I never took the time to think of it. Looking around now, this all seems pretty ideal. It's actually everything I might have described if you'd asked me yesterday. It's just..."

Edgar didn't finish. His speech was cut short by the sound of his glass shattering against the floor and the legs of his chair scraping violently backward as he turned and began to dash across the hall.

It fluttered just before him; silver against gold. He pushed angels aside as he went, hearing behind him surprised squeals interlaced with joyous acknowledgments of his passing. Edgar jumped up and down as he went, struggling to keep track of her movements—this angel wrapped in her mirror-like dress.

Bev, he somehow knew, despite how foolish the idea seemed. When had he seen her last? He couldn't even say now. *Not since the old days at The Scholar anyway.*

Bev had been, well, Edgar never was very effective at articulating what Bev had been. *A girl I knew—the girl.* No matter who she was, Edgar was certain she was exactly who he needed now.

As his feet pounded over the dark wooden floor of the Golden Ballroom, white puffs of fog billowed up from under them. Like lightning, she flashed, ever just beyond reach. But he was certain now, while before he'd only suspected, and as the fog began to fill the hall and envelop him, he fixed his attention on her, stitching his eyes to the silver of her dress. Behind him, the rest slipped from view.

Suddenly, there she was. The fog held her in its embrace, cradling her as if this was its sole purpose. In all the unworld where Edgar stood, it was just him and her and the transcendental white fog.

"Bev," he said, only to find he had no follow-up. She was not a tall woman, but her brooding amber eyes still held a tunnel to some reality where the world made more sense; where the confusions and temptations that had surrounded him daily since they'd parted just vanished, allowing for a comfort he could now hardly recall.

Nothing about her was especially remarkable. She had plain, straight brown hair reaching to her back, a round face, and a patient—if occasionally exasperated—smile was ever etched upon her thin lips. It was there even now, setting him instantly at peace.

"Oh Edgar, what happened?" Her voice was soft, a whisper spoken from one pillow to another, for Edgar's ears alone.

"I don't know." Edgar hung his head, relieved that the ballroom was gone as he stood before this memory made flesh.

"What did you do?" Bev asked. Her expression told him she already knew. She always did.

"I…thought I had more time."

"You always did." Her words cut, and Edgar's throat was dry.

"I'm sorry." He was. It hadn't occurred to him until just then. The silence was overwhelming and his stomach rolled over like a submissive whelp.

"I know." Her voice held a boundless tone of understanding. He'd missed Bev, though he'd never admitted it. There was so much he wanted to ask; so much he knew he should explain. But his head spun, and again he could vaguely hear the echoing bass of the hall. He quickly determined that he needed another drink, at the least, if he was to sufficiently steady his nerve.

Bev stood patiently; she'd always had to wait on Edgar. He stammered dumbly, searching for words. None came. There was so much to say, so many things to offer; but as each one played through his mind, Edgar's spine trembled, and he swallowed instinctively as he pulled hard from his dying cigarette.

Bev always had all the answers—until she didn't. She'd been a lighthouse for Edgar's reckless voyages, faithfully promising to illuminate the way back to safe harbour. Then one day her light went out, and Edgar tacitly understood that it had been his own failing in its upkeep. "What do we do now?" he asked.

His legs were shaking, and a sudden wave of nausea threatened to topple him as he lost himself in her searching eyes. He longed for answers. He wanted to hide, to escape. He needed a fucking drink, a barrel, an ocean of booze to dive in and drown everything pressing in on him, demanding accountability and responsibility and all those things which Edgar Vincent never could abide.

The music was back now, and before Bev's light, the fog was recoiling once again, promising Edgar deliverance from the treacherous seas he'd set his prow to mere minutes ago.

"Anything..."

It wasn't her voice. Not her tongue that slid over those shining lips as she spoke.

"...You want!"

These weren't Bev's words. *Not Bev at all.*

He reeled backwards, the music and the smoke and the booze slamming back and forth in his skull as he opened his eyes to find he was lying prostrate upon the big, curved couch beside the small table. Tyra, barely clothed now, was licking his neck as if seeking sustenance, and Leslie was considerate enough to place another fresh scotch into his desperately searching hand.

"It wasn't just BHI," Edgar blurted in a staccato stutter. "I was finally finding my direction..."

The lines of light were smearing like old sidewalk chalk, and Tyra's tongue was working its way down as her hands moved with acrobatic deftness upon his belt.

"I know I haven't been what I should, but I was working on it. If I'd had a bit more time..."

That his jacket was unzipped was to be expected while indoors, but that his shirt was also unbuttoned did come as a surprise as he felt Tyra's teeth teasing their way down his broad chest.

"They say I could be more. Well, Duncan does. No one else bothers. But I know it's true. I only wanted to contribute, to offer what I could. But you've gotta make a choice; either be yourself or be like everyone else. I won't do that. I know what they say about me, but I work for what I want. I push harder than anyone, and damn them for judging me for it. Stupid Duncan." Edgar slurred and stammered, but around him, the angels listened intently, supportive smiles on their beautiful faces.

"Everyone leaves or says it's too late—too late to turn it around. But I've been more consistent than anyone. You know what you get, what I am. At least I'm honest!"

Tyra was significantly lower than his chest now, but Edgar was beyond being surprised. As he revealed himself to the hollow things around him, his nakedness seemed only fitting.

"Now it's all done. I don't know why I'm here, what I did to earn it. Who I saved, or... I remember walking, searching... I remember that building." The memory danced before him, just on the edge of consciousness.

"I remember how long it seemed, that walk, and falling, and how fucking lonely it felt in the end. Fuck it though. It's too late now. I know they're right; I'm as bad as they all say. But, I just needed a bit more time."

Tyra was moving upon him like a piston now, and things were looking up. Edgar struggled to figure out what else he wanted to say, but realized it wasn't worth the effort. His head throbbed, and he knew he would have one hell of a hangover the following day.

But tonight, tonight Edgar would be in heaven.

CHAPTER 4
THE PERSONAL STUDY

Edgar had never been the sort of man to repeat a mistake, nor to fail in learning crucial lessons. Even in the hardest times of his life—the competition for which was steep, to say the least—Edgar found that despite the suffering caused by his misdeeds, there was also great knowledge to be gained from the experience.

It was a useful philosophy. When, in the long climb to relevance in the film scoring industry, he realized he'd chosen the wrong project or misread the director's intentions, Edgar was always able to find a suitable solution. By simply taking some quick mental notes and employing a little bit of his trademark social finesse, he managed to consistently come out more or less unscathed.

On one particularly unsettling Saturday, he'd found himself at an unknown club, already deep into flirting with an especially enticing beauty. Upon inquiring about her life, he'd discovered that she was, in fact, the young daughter of one of his biggest contracts.

Such concerns would certainly overwhelm any normal man, but not Edgar. With his keen insight and unwavering will, he had merely vowed—as he ushered the bewildered lady out of his studio apartment the next morning—to avoid revealing his name henceforth.

Of course, being more efficient than most men, he'd often gone above and beyond this particular goal by simply avoiding asking his ladies' names to begin with.

Once, more recently than Edgar cared to admit, he'd been walking with traffic along a freeway, desperately waving his thumb in hopes of finding a ride out of the derelict neighbourhood where he'd awoken. Instead, he found himself picked up by a police cruiser. A life-changing moment for some perhaps, but Edgar was no typical man. So, after thoroughly scrubbing the ink from his fingertips and calling a friend *(Emeric, the judgemental shit)* for a ride home, Edgar reflected deeply upon the caper and resolved for the future to hitchhike only when walking against traffic.

This had proven successful, and never again did the police manage to catch old Edgar unawares—at least not for hitchhiking.

In his career, his leisure time, and even in his love life, Edgar never passed up an opportunity to improve his station. So, having been hurt twice at this point by his beloved Scottish mistress, he knew in his heart it was due time to seek solace in the arms of another fair lady.

"Hello, Brandy!" Edgar exclaimed, pouring himself a generous glass of the fragrant elixir.

Bold and independent, Edgar may have been a man eager to learn from his mistakes, but that was certainly not to say he was a stranger to adversity. So, upon waking once again with a raging hangover, he wasted no time coming up with a solution for the dry pain that encompassed his being. *Hair of the dog*, he acknowledged, sending a rush of brandy coursing down his throat.

That morning had been a trying ordeal. Not an unfamiliar experience by any stretch, Edgar had awoken in the comfort of his own bed, with only the vaguest recollections from the night before spinning through his head like the illuminations of a child's bedside mobile.

The renewal of his hangover had admittedly been disappointing. *Even in heaven?* he'd lamented, only to find himself suddenly wondering whether or not the entire affair had been nothing more than a dismal nightmare.

It took several minutes of careful contemplation before Edgar, having slowly cobbled together a functional approximation of the night's events, rolled over to find his bed unoccupied. Tyra, who at least he was entirely convinced had accompanied him from the Golden Ballroom, was now conspicuously absent.

So, this is heaven, he accepted immediately.

After pulling his scattered clothing back on and quickly checking the contents of his pockets, he began his journey out of the bedroom, down the short hallway and into his esteemed study: the other of only two rooms in his home from which he took any true pleasure. Finding it in order, Edgar faced yet another existential dilemma. *What does a man do in heaven?*

Often enough, he knew, the answer to one question depended on another; and the more pertinent question was, he supposed, *what fucking day is it, anyway?*

The surreal nature of the question was not lost on a man of Edgar's acumen, and as he pressed his fingers to his temples to still the painful cacophony in his skull, he found his answer quite naturally. *Sure as hell feels like a Sunday*, he decided.

It was the best answer he could come up with and, since his death precluded the chance of his having any legitimate business to do, Sunday indeed seemed to be the fitting choice.

Of course, Edgar was a bright man and never one to miss a promising pattern. Based on what he'd experienced to this point, on top of the fact that he was indeed dead, it seemed reasonable to assume that tomorrow would be a Sunday as well. Therefore, with another long sip of his brandy, he resolved to be prepared.

Every day is Sunday in this place. Doesn't that just fucking figure?

Edgar's study was a large, open space that dominated the greater portion of his apartment. Its purpose was two-fold, serving both as a place for relaxation and reflection, as well as being the focal point of his musical efforts. All of his most prized possessions were displayed proudly along the walls. His first studio-quality guitar (a standard red and white Squire), his best guitar (a classic black and white Telecaster), and his sexiest guitar (a curvy Les Paul with a beautiful light wood finish), hung as the centrepieces of the study, directly behind his main desk. Continuing out in both directions from this point, the equipment wrapped the majority of the room. There was a Fender Precision Bass, a 12-String guitar, several acoustics, a collection of horns, tambourines, and myriad other exotic instruments acquired over the years to fill out his collection.

There was also an old keytar kept less for function and more as a conversation starter with the drunken hangers-on Edgar often brought home. They tended to care less about music and more about kitsch.

In the corner directly across from his bedroom hall was Edgar's mixing station. Or, stations rather. Indeed, Edgar's study featured two separate mixing stations—for very different sorts of mixing. The first was a simple refrigerator and bar set-up, with a short end-table for the assembly of more demanding drinks. This had been among the first additions made when Edgar moved into the apartment and of late it had taken the lion's share of his time from the other, more legitimate mixing station.

Setting the brandy decanter back down on the bar, Edgar turned and let his finger run along the edge of the big, wood-paneled Roland Jupiter-80 synthesizer that was the main hub of his professional mixing station. This sat to the right of a comfortable office chair that was enclosed on three sides by tables bearing complex arrays of studio equipment. A computer with several monitors was at the centre, surrounded entirely by mounted speakers and boards full of dials, buttons, sliders, knobs, and flashing lights. There was a big old amp to the left, along with a second keyboard, an expensive set of drum pads, and a litany of other gadgets used to perfect the tunes he created. Lifting his hand away, Edgar noticed a thin layer of dust on the tip of his finger. After a quick sip of brandy, he sighed, recalling how alive he'd always felt whenever he sat in his little musical cockpit, letting his hands fly deftly from one instrument to the next as he dreamed up creative new ways to make all the disparate sounds come together into a beautiful and comprehensive whole.

There was no doubt about it, when Edgar got down to business and applied himself to his craft, he was a spectacle to behold. Bouncing from one instrument to the next, he'd swivel about in his chair jotting notes, turning dials, and moving his fingers in the air as if conducting an invisible orchestra. The solitary nature of his work sometimes came as a surprise to those who didn't know him well, but Edgar never tired of explaining that when it was just him and the silence, he always felt that his potential had no bounds.

The dust now lining his studio, however, served as a discouraging reminder of the artistic struggles he'd been experiencing of late.

Directly beside the Jupiter-80 was his "other" mixing station—a pairing which he'd found especially convenient during sleepless nights struggling to get a piece just right. The comparably pristine and dustless condition of the latter did little to lighten his mood.

Maybe a bit of artistic release would be the ticket, he thought. But his splitting headache and endless doubts didn't make for the most productive mood, and Edgar reasoned that he'd be better off getting his head straight before he tried to exert himself in any meaningful way. So, with the contents of the half-empty glass in his hand sloshing about, he stumbled over to sit at his main desk at the far end of the room.

The desk itself had been a present from his parents upon the completion of his music theory degree. Heavy and simple, it occupied the far end of his office like the altar of some ancient cathedral. Its surface was empty and made from dark mahogany. The desk was a special point of pride for Edgar, being the primary locale in which he conceived most of his great ideas, celebrated his most significant successes, and often sat, alone and silent, to contemplate the crucial choices of his life.

Was Chanel here too? I hope I didn't pass her up for that wanton idiot Tyra, he wondered, taking a seat.

The sudden grin that tore across Edgar's face tested his throbbing head, but did nothing to deter his intentions as he shifted his weight and snatched his phone from his pocket.

"Time to update old Emeric," he declared, "that little pervert will definitely want to know about this."

Flipping instinctually through his contacts, Edgar's eyes flitted apathetically over the names on their way down to his target: Alexis, Alicia, Anastasia, Anita, Barbara, Bella, Brenda, Candy ($), Christi, Christie (Redhead), Chevon, Debra (DON'T ANSWER!!!), Denise... There he was, Dirty Emmy.

Like a who's who list of aspiring models—and inevitable porn stars. Edgar laughed to himself and took another long draw of brandy.

With Emeric's number lighting up his screen, he paused. Frowning, Edgar understood that the voice on the other end of the line would be nothing more than a projection of his own expectations, which made the actual act of calling seem rather redundant. He could already imagine exactly how the conversation would go.

"Hi, Edgar."

"Emeric, you vile son-of-a-bitch, what's up?"

"Not much, I'm just..."

"Shut up Emeric, I know what you're wondering."

"Edgar, I really don't..."

"Shh, it's OK. Some of us live life fully, and others just live it vicariously. It's alright, my friend. So, you remember those angels I went to see?"

His musings trailed off into obscurity at this point, his own memory of the night being almost as spotty as it was for the Saturday before...

Shit, he recalled. The manner of his death was no clearer than it had been the night prior.

His brandy glass was empty now and Edgar realized with great regret that he'd left the decanter on the bar next to his synthesizer at the far end of his study.

But Edgar's attention to detail was as keen as his respect for ritual, and in the bottom right drawer of his desk, he knew there was an unopened bottle of scotch awaiting him.

Leaning back into the soft leather of his chair, he considered his options. The scotch had been purchased in—admittedly premature—preparation for the completion of his BHI work. It would, of course, now go uncompleted.

Opening the desk drawer, Edgar pushed aside his ragged old tie and let his finger run along the dusty bottle of scotch.

How long has it been here? he wondered.

The mixing station seemed a world away, and the scotch at hand was superb, but BHI was the project Edgar had waited for his whole life. It was going to cement his legacy, prove to the world what he was made of. Somehow, he realized with a defeated sigh, it seemed unfitting to open the bottle under false pretenses.

And so, with an exaggerated show of anguish, Edgar forced himself wearily back across his study, retrieved the decanter of brandy, and returned to his desk. Filling his glass once more, he took a long chug, then pulled his pack of cigarettes out from under him.

The unexpected was, for Edgar, quite mundane at this point—the shocking rather blasé. Depravity, revulsion, and perversion were all so very commonplace that it was exceedingly rare for anything at all to give him pause. Yet when he opened his packet to find a single vacant space—its emptiness glaring at him like a hole through midnight—the turn of his stomach caught Edgar entirely off guard, very nearly making him spill his previous night's sins all over his custom desk.

Was my office always this dark? he wondered as the flame of his lighter sparked to life then quickly died, leaving him alone in a room which had never before felt so very lonely.

Heaven, Edgar concluded, *may still take some getting used to.*

It's certainly not what I'd always been told, he admitted. Aside from the golden gate and that sly devil Pete, he could still hardly believe this utopia of extravagance and excess was the same place his Nana had so often warned him about missing out on.

"I must at least get some credit for the improvements," he quipped. But no snide chuckles came in answer, and already Edgar felt he was back in another Sunday entirely.

*****

He could feel the tight black suit biting at the flesh of his young neck, and the hard, cold wood of the pew tried his youthful impatience. There was no escape. As the preacher droned on about confession and repentance, Edgar knew he was thoroughly and inescapably penned in. His mother sat stoically at his left side—wearing finer clothes than Rosa Vasquez-Vincent had ever in her life imagined she would wear. An absolute picture of elegance, Edgar could remember admiring her beauty even then. To his right, offering him sharp elbows and dull observations, sat Nana Vasquez.

"Listen to me little Edito, these words will save you," he remembered his

Nana saying to him at the start of Mass each week. Old and weary, the woman always spoke as if her point were coming to her a moment too late, and with her strong Argentinian accent, was ever an imposing source of insight.

"Everything will be OK, my dear," she'd promised time and again, "just as long as you have faith."

*****

Taking a final sip, Edgar flinched, feeling anew the cruel rap of his Nana's elbow against his young ribs. His glass was empty again, and he grinned eagerly as he remedied that problem.

Nana Vasquez had been his mother's mother. Edgar had never known his father's parents. In fact, he occasionally reflected when deep in his cups, he'd never been entirely certain he'd known the man himself.

Edgar remembered his father as much for the painfully long absences as for the occasional appearances he would make; showing up with little notice, but much fanfare. Each time, he came bearing some extravagant new instrument for Edgar to learn and some incredible business news to share with Rosa. Then he would vanish again into the night, chasing some unreachable deadline.

Despite the occasional elbow, his mother and grandmother—whether regaling him with delicious family recipes, teaching him about their faith, or reminding him how very lucky he was to have a father who worked so hard—had been constant sources of strength to a young Edgar Vincent. To this day, he could think of only a handful of people who'd ever known him so well.

And he had known them in turn. If Edgar had never felt entirely at peace in the tall towered church he seemed to have spent so much of his childhood in, the women who perpetually surrounded him within it were the very meaning of comfort…of home.

Faith: it wasn't just some word to be bandied about on Sunday. Not to them. They lived it daily. In their words, in their actions, even in their unflinching reverence for his father Eli.

More than any of that, however, it was his mother and grandmother's faith in Edgar himself that stuck with him after all the years. No doubt it was partially due to his being an only child, but their esteem for him had known no limits. Edgar—their golden boy, their "rayo de sol". Certainly, guidance and scolding had abounded in their presence, for despite their humility, there was much they wished to share. But Edgar was a quick learner, and the unflappable power he had to melt their hearts with a smile and shrug was his easiest lesson.

No matter how far he strayed, Edgar always knew that a quick confession of guilt and a sly profession of love would suffice to bring them back to his side. Their Edgar, their little prince. *Everything will be OK...*

Edgar finished his cigarette, lit another, and took a long drink.

...Just as long as you have faith.

On occasion, Edgar wondered if the unconditional nature of their love may have spoiled him somewhat, for he often found the real world—the adult world—quite lacking in comparison.

Well, thank Christ for heaven!

Only once since leaving home had Edgar found such inherent, inscrutable love. A single period when he'd felt his failures were entirely immaterial to a person he was certain would never forsake him.

Edgar stared into the silver sheen of his lighter, never seeing himself in its mirror-like reflection.

Bev...

Even in his rare private introspections, he had trouble putting into words exactly what Bev had meant to him. It may have been that he felt some shame about his naivety in the matter or perhaps it was just natural human aversion to opening up old scar tissue. Whatever it was, he was seldom challenged on it, and he allowed himself to reflect on those times in only the most solemn— and inevitably intoxicated—of moods. Even then...*it has been a while.*

It wasn't a pining, definitely not a lust. He was certain there remained no embers of what used to simmer between them. It was an age ago, a childish thing...

When Edgar and Duncan had packed their belongings and driven off in a rental van to attend university, Duncan had quickly maneuvered himself into a prestigious circle of aspiring young lawyers, working to build the connections needed for a successful career in law. Edgar, meanwhile, had met Bev.

It hadn't been a long relationship. Indeed, the year it did last was a striking testament to the inherently patient and forgiving nature of Bev. In Edgar, Bev saw everything that he saw in himself. The spirit, the incredible artistic potential, and the endless sense of rousing fun supplied only by men of Edgar's passions.

In Bev, Edgar had found everything he'd been promised as a child. Their relationship had never been easy, as even in this most dedicated period of his life, keeping his attention took significant effort. The further he delved into his artistic ambitions, the deeper he burrowed into the offbeat and rebellious lifestyle he so closely associated with such brilliance—and on that excavation, in particular, Edgar very nearly struck magma.

Yet for every indiscretion, Edgar received clemency, and for every absent night, he was greeted only with comfort. Bev stood by him with a fierce dedication, and for a while, he had felt those old words were true—that no matter what befell him, whether by the cruelty of chance or the inevitability of poor choices—everything would be alright.

Finishing the drink in his hand, he poured himself another with a reluctant smirk. He didn't take the time to remember those days often enough, although he never failed to credit them as being among his most formative. After all, it had been the year he'd met two of his greatest friends: Emeric and Alex.

That year too, he reflected as he puffed on his smoke, had marked several other key moments in the young life of Edgar Vincent. It had been that year—the first week of it in fact—that he had achieved his first true blackout. He'd gotten into his first bar fight as well; his first dozen actually, if memory served. The blackout, of course, had been far from an isolated incident, and so there was every possibility that memory did not serve at all.

Edgar had composed his first original song that year—a languorous keyboard sonata—for Bev. It had served as an apology for his first ever infidelity.

Cherished above all those other memories, however, it had also been his first year at The Scholar's Lament. Edgar and Bev, Duncan and Alex. Even the weaselly little Emeric would pull his beak-like nose out of his books long enough to join them for their ritualistic meet-up every second Saturday.

Jake hadn't shown up until the following year. When he did appear, he'd merely been a local high-school kid with a fake ID and a desperate hunger for college girls. Much to the disappointment of the rest of his peers, Edgar had quickly developed a deep fascination with Jake, and proved eager to take the big oaf under his wing.

Jake had never really gotten to know Bev. By then, Edgar reminisced, lighting another smoke as he stared suspiciously into the still empty space in his packet, Bev had been showing up with less and less reliability. In his drunken reflections at the time, it had seemed to Edgar that she'd finally lost faith.

But that was so many years ago. So many decisions, so many women, so very, very many drinks.

Edgar took a moment to top up his brandy. The painful memories bouncing around in his head were doing little to still the ghosts of the previous night's drinking, and his hangover was a supernova in the empty spaces of his mind.

Heaven, he ultimately decided, *is no place to waste on memories.* This realm, to the best of his understanding, answered to him—and at that moment, Edgar felt about ready to take full advantage of the fact.

The lingering question is—how?

It was hardly a difficult question to face. Any man who complained about the opportunity to do anything he wanted, anytime he wanted, must certainly lack any respectable sense of imagination as far as Edgar was concerned. And if Edgar lacked anything, imagination was not it.

The first idea, however, proved to be a trap, as his immediate urge to pursue booze and women promised only to reinforce his cyclic course. *Earthly desires,* Edgar lamented.

He had half a mind to go see Jake. But considering the shenanigans the dastardly duo had achieved on Earth, Edgar paled to imagine the heinous shit they would get up to without the concerns of the mortal coil.

Alex, however, seemed a more fitting choice. While never the partner in crime Jake had been, Alex was always the de facto source any time Edgar felt compelled to…open his mind.

If he was to sit down with Alex now, Edgar was certain they would end up waxing philosophic and almost certainly manage to hammer out the finer points of Edgar's increasingly esoteric existence.

But it was Edgar's head that hammered now. The marching band he'd assembled shot by shot the night prior still pounded out its rhythm through his sorry skull, and he wondered if some nice, grounded advice might be what the doctor ordered. If so, then Emeric was most certainly the right choice.

Edgar poured another drink, disposed of it briskly, and then poured another. *One more time, if you'd be so kind,* he joked to himself. Consistency, after all, was a trait even old Emmy would endorse.

He gazed about his old study. It was exactly as he'd left it, if perhaps a little dimmer. Turning his attention for a moment to the ceiling, he searched for any lights that needed replacing, before chuckling shamefully to himself. *Hardly a task befitting the situation,* he decided.

Heaven, it was clear, was at least as wondrous as promised. To have reality bend to one's own imagination was a gift beyond value. Still, an old memory cautioned him: "When we live according to our basest desires, it's easy to miss out on life entirely."

But there was no need to worry himself with such quandaries now. Not when good friends and good times were only a thought away. *After all,* Edgar insisted, *this is heaven, and I'm meant to be celebrating the life I've lived.* With that attitude, he was certain everything else would be just fine.

At least, he conceded, putting away the rest of his drink with authority— *I'll have to have faith.*

CHAPTER 5
THE IGNOBLE DRIVE

When Edgar was just a small child, his father Eli had once returned from a business trip with a little, hand-crafted guitar for the young boy. Then he left, back to work, back to earn all those things Edgar was so often told he took for granted.

Only a few short days after his father departed, his mother Rosa swore that Edgar was going to drive her mad with his constant playing. There was no doubt her concerns were valid. Edgar had attacked the guitar with a voracious, unquenchable drive toward mastery. Without lessons or any clear instruction, he had been determined to find his own way.

From running the strings along various household objects to create new tones—and plenty of unwanted scuffs throughout the home—to putting on his best Bruce Springsteen sneer and slamming his soft hands against the strings until they were raw, his efforts were certainly admirable. In fact, there was no denial from anyone who saw the growing boy claw ever deeper into his passion, Edgar was driven.

It was a quality he'd never entirely lost. Nothing brought a smile to his cherubic little face quite like creating from amongst his growing collection of instruments, the perfect sound to accompany a moment and bring it to life in his youthful mind.

That remained true until the early years of middle school, when this very drive led him to bring his guitar to school and inadvertently discover the effect a moody rock star could have on a naïve young girl.

Rosa prayed long and hard that night. Edgar laid damp towels under his door to muffle the sound of his practicing well into the next morning.

It was this drive, also, which had pushed Edgar to such a respectable position in his chosen field; and it's discovered effect, which fuelled most every other endeavour in his life.

He drove strange women mad; he drove familiar lovers to tears. Whenever Edgar laid eyes on something he wanted, his drive to realize that dream was a fire beyond quenching.

"Where are we going?" The voice was Duncan's—deep and measured, with a wry confidence that could make any lesser man question even his most deeply-held convictions.

From between his legs, Edgar raised a small silver flask to his lips and held it overlong. Finally, he let it down, and with a rumbling sigh accompanied by a dragon's tail of cigarette smoke, gazed around him.

The orange ember of his cigarette was reflected back by the curve of the windshield in front of him, and in the open glove box at his knees waited a cornucopia of high-end mini-bottles ready to replenish his flask whenever it ran dry.

Empty fields and tall trees raced past through the window to his right, and before him, a highway stretched off toward an indefinable point where it presumed to meet the cloudless blue sky.

"I think we're there already," Edgar groaned, sinking down into the plush embrace of a leather seat as he shielded his face from the sun's cruel rays. Beside him, Duncan rolled his piercing green eyes, and a curl of his mouth drew a peevish line along his strong jaw.

Edgar squirmed. Disappointing Duncan never pleased him, although the regular practice he got did soften the blow. Still, he searched quickly about for clues, imagining that somewhere in the vast expanses of nothing before him, there must surely be some hint as to where his mind had taken them.

Fucking heaven…can't they just make it easy? Edgar wondered with a scowl. Duncan had been his goal; at least that much was right. He'd ultimately left his study in search of Duncan, he knew, because his oldest friend was the most likely to understand his present ordeal.

"I ran into Bev." Edgar spoke the words around the lip of his flask. Of late, Duncan had in truth become something of a drag, always lecturing him about the significance of his choices. But, Edgar reasoned, being that he was now dead, and in heaven to boot, surely the days of Duncan's righteous indignation had come to an end.

"I thought you might." Duncan's eyes never left the road ahead of him. Dilapidated barns and quaint little houses blurred by, and Edgar frowned.

I didn't, he thought. He lit another cigarette. From his package, the empty space stared back at him like a dark alley eager for an uninitiated stranger.

"Why would you think that?" he asked.

"Edgar," Duncan said with a smirk, "who do you think you're talking to?"

"Myself—for all the answers you're giving."

"You didn't come here for answers."

Edgar despised Duncan's ability to manipulate a conversation almost as fiercely as he adored it in himself.

"The reunion was...less than I might have imagined."

Why had he believed Duncan could help him? They were lifelong friends and knew things about one another that would surely sunder most brothers. Yet Edgar couldn't deny they'd grown apart during university. *Increasingly so as time rolled on,* he knew, *exponentially even.*

Duncan was as driven as Edgar—one of the few. Sadly, their drives took them in very different directions, from incredibly contrary origins. Their opposing journeys had eclipsed long ago.

"So," Duncan spoke, his voice as measured and even as ever, "where are we going?"

Ever the goddamn pragmatist. Duncan had, in Edgar's esteemed opinion, always been overly focused on the destination at the expense of the journey. It hadn't always mattered. In their youth, the destination had been sufficiently distant to make their shared journey a satisfying smorgasbord of all the things Edgar had continued to cherish to his bitter end.

But at some point...

Suddenly, the endless fields and all-encompassing sky were no longer the inscrutable clues they were a moment before.

Edgar knew exactly where he was.

*****

"So, where are we going?" Duncan had asked.

Edgar, sitting on the passenger side of the long bench seat in their rented U-Haul, did not respond. Instead, he stole another quick pull from the shiny silver flask nestled on the bench between them and let out a long, contented sigh as he ran his fingers again along the supple sleeves of his new leather jacket.

Earlier that day, Edgar had left his childhood home to enter this U-Haul van with Duncan on a one-way trip to the rest of their lives.

His father Eli had left him with a solemn head nod and a firm handshake.

Rosa, his mother, had offered a prayer.

It didn't matter. Only the day before, Edgar had dipped deep into his line of credit and treated himself to a graduation gift more befitting his nascent lifestyle.

So, as he left home with his new brown jacket hung loosely about his broad shoulders and his Squire guitar slung lazily across his back, Edgar was certain the future had in store for him a direct and expedient voyage to everything he'd ever imagined.

"Touch it. Just feel how soft and smooth it is," Edgar demanded, extending his leather-swaddled arm across the cab of the van towards Duncan.

"I've turned you down on far less provocative requests, Mr. Vincent," Duncan answered with a smirk.

"I fucking told you not to call me that!" Edgar snapped, lighting a cigarette from his near-empty pack. "Dammit, out again! We're gonna have to find a store soon."

"Well, you've got the map, genius. I know we're nearly at my pass-off point anyway, so you'd better slow down."

Edgar glanced at the torn and crinkled map lodged into the space between his seat and the door. Being the bright and enterprising young men they were, Edgar and Duncan had spent the past week poring over the map and dividing the route to university into long stretches of alternatingly coloured lines. One man would drive as the other drank, with the carefully plotted map allowing time to prevent the risk of a drunk driver, while also circumventing the abysmal idea of an entirely sober road-trip.

"I still can't believe we couldn't make room for my guitar up front." Edgar tried to change the subject.

"You've already bent enough rules," Duncan scolded, casting a sage glare Edgar's way.

How does he know? Clever bastard! Edgar had allotted himself space for only a single instrument—his guitar—in the van, but had at the last minute deemed it necessary to sneak his keyboard into a blanket roll.

"You're just jealous," said Edgar.

"Jealous?"

"Duncan, I know I'm not the wingman you deserve; definitely not what you need. But I can't help how I look, and if my handsomeness causes you envy, I truly am sorry."

Duncan allowed himself an annoyed laugh. "I forgive you, mon frère, but you do need to get on top of that map and let me know where we're at."

Working to conceal a discouraged pout, Edgar grabbed up the map while taking a cursory glance at the road signs blurring by.

The reality that met him was a bitter pill. His turn at the wheel was only fifteen minutes straight up the road, and he was, much to his chagrin, certainly still sober enough to assume driving duties.

There should be a store at our waypoint, Edgar imagined, *but…*

"Turn up here!" he blurted.

"There, into that field?" Duncan was baffled. "Is that really where you're pointing? I'm not sure that little strip is even a road. It looks more like a game trail."

"It's a shortcut." Edgar's tone rose only slightly as he spoke, "Besides, I need to get to a store."

"Whatever you say, Captain," Duncan agreed reluctantly.

Edgar sank back into the dirty cloth seat and smiled, taking another greedy pull from their flask.

*****

Now Edgar watched the fields fly by through the window. Cows munched hungrily on grass as sparse clusters of trees passed slowly in the distance. A rickety old barbed wire fence slid along at their side.

He shivered.

"I still don't even know how I died, you know," he moaned listlessly.

"You're dead, Edgar, does the how really matter?"

Edgar shot a scathing look at his old friend. "Yeah, it does actually."

"Why?"

"What the fuck do you even mean? How am I supposed to move forward if I don't even know what the hell happened to get me here?"

"Well, I suppose you could start by answering my question."

Edgar puffed at his smoke, took another drink from his flask, and raised one eyebrow inquisitively.

"Where are we going?" Duncan repeated himself a third time. Edgar shrugged and chuckled sardonically.

"You know, the world would be a lot brighter for you if you'd stop speaking every idiotic thought you have, and start saying what you really mean," said Duncan, keeping his eyes on the road.

"Shut up," said Edgar. Digging into his jacket, he produced a pair of stylish sunglasses and slipped them on his face just in time to conceal the roll of his eyes.

"The timing of it is what gets me the most," Edgar continued with his gaze locked upon the distant horizon. "Of all the times to die! Why did I have to go just before finally completing BHI? I mean, with even a few more months, I could have at least had something worthwhile to leave behind. It's fucking bullshit!"

The silence hung in the car for an uncomfortable minute before Edgar turned to meet Duncan's gaze. An incredulous expression was painted on his friend's face.

"Edgar," Duncan spoke slowly, choosing his words with measured care. "How long have I listened to you talk about this project and how close you are to finishing it? How many years has it been?"

Edgar only scowled, offering no answer. Taking a gladiatorial chug from his flask, he held it out to Duncan, who shrugged it off with a nod towards his hands on the wheel.

Finally, Edgar broke the tension. "It was hardly even a year that I was with Bev. Why weren't you more surprised when I told you I saw her?"

Duncan just shook his head, providing no explanation. His eyes were glued to the road. Looking up, Edgar again took in the empty miles before him: the fields and the bridges, the off-ramps, and pastures.

He'd seen them all before.

*****

"Check this out, I have a surprise!" Edgar had beamed, pulling a crumpled sheet from his pocket as the old van rumbled down the gravel back roads. "I did some research, made some calls. I have here a list of every bar within walking distance of campus, along with actual testimonials and interviews with patrons as to the...clientele we might encounter. We are golden! The future truly is blessed, my friend."

"That's wonderful Eds, and I'll be happy to attend each one of them with you, if we ever get there. We've been driving these damn trails for hours now, where the hell are we going?"

Edgar didn't answer immediately—preoccupied with refilling their empty flask from the big discount bottle of whiskey stashed under the seat. "I'm sure it's just up here a bit. Calm down and listen to all these options: Rowdy's, Lush, The Scholar's Lament, Ye Olde Watering Hole; it'll take us a lifetime to visit all these!" Taking a quick nip from the flask and stealing a smoke from Duncan's pack, he considered for a moment. "Well, a damn good weekend at the very least."

"Is that really all you're excited about? Bars and girls? I enjoy them as much as you do bud, but there's a lot more to look forward to than that. None of that shit is even new to you. What about all the rest?"

"Well, I also found a place nearby where we should be able to get a Slip-n-Slide."

53

Duncan gaped.

"I have a plan," Edgar assuaged him with a devilish grin. Duncan didn't seem encouraged. "Besides, they're all new bars. All new girls! And yes, of course, there's our mutual rise to fame and glory to look forward to, but that just goes without saying. Still," he finished with a hurt tone in his voice, "there's no need to halt the hype train before it even leaves the station."

"Fair enough," Duncan acquiesced, reaching into his pack for a cigarette, only to find it empty. Shooting a frustrated glare at Edgar, he instead snatched the shiny flask from his mooching friend and emptied it in two triumphant chugs. "Although I might argue this train is well out of the station and thoroughly lost in the wilderness at this point."

"Get off that sauce, you damnable lunatic!" Edgar's faux-panic brought a smile to both of their faces. "You haven't even gotten us safely to your waypoint yet." He promptly set to work at refilling the flask, spilling whiskey all over his jeans in the effort. He couldn't help but smirk. *Crazy Duncan, can't even wait his turn.*

Edgar had always admired Duncan's reckless spirit. Calm and focused, yet so wanton and mad at the same time. *Almost enough to make a guy feel bad... I'm definitely too drunk to drive now, even if we manage to find our way,* he chuckled giddily to himself. *He's going to be so pissed if he ever gets us back on track.*

"I do mean it though Edgar—when we live according to our basest desires, it's easy to miss out on life entirely. This move is a turning point; you've got to keep your eyes on the track."

"Says the guy who just scoffed at my intensive research and planning?"

"You could've handled all of that with half the effort. Besides, there's more to it. I've been thinking a lot about this Eds—about what I want from life. Fame and fortune is all well and good, but leaving home now, it's time to consider how to build our own, you know? Don't you ever think about those things?"

Edgar sipped slowly from the flask, staring into its silver surface in quiet contemplation before finally answering. "Tsk tsk, you're getting old, pal. Families and responsibilities? Yeah, no shit I want those. But you're putting the garnish before the cocktail here. You've only got one life, my friend. You've got to enjoy it. All that other stuff will come in due time." Edgar turned to his friend with a caricatured grin. "You've just got to have faith."

*****

It all seems like a lifetime ago.

Edgar bit his lip at the irony of this admission. The interior of the car had been quiet for a while now—Edgar lost in his silent ruminations, Duncan fixated on the road ahead.

Finally, Edgar shifted in his seat, his old leather jacket creaking against the fresh cushions. Removing his sunglasses, he was surprised to find how dark the world outside had grown.

"Jesus, where did the time go?"

As he cast a sidelong look at Edgar, the hint of a smile played across Duncan's smooth-shaven face. "Do they use that word up here?"

"Time?" Edgar asked with a grin, and the two old friends shared an uncomfortable laugh.

"You're still wondering about her, aren't you?" Duncan always had an uncanny ability to read the writing on the walls of Edgar's silences.

"I hadn't for years," he answered honestly. "I still can't imagine why she would show up here, of all places."

"What do you mean?"

"This is heaven, isn't it?"

Duncan only waited.

"So, aren't I supposed to be happy here? What was the point? Just to complicate things and stress me out? Shit, would it kill them to give a dead man a bit of peace?"

"Eds, buddy," Duncan shifted behind the wheel, "what were you looking for when you left us at The Scholar?"

"What?" The incredulity in Edgar's voice was venomous. "Maybe you can't relate with your perfect—still ongoing—life, but I was kind of busy reeling with the news of my recent demise."

"So," Duncan pushed, maintaining the patient pace of his voice. "What were you looking for?"

"For distraction, I guess. Shit! For fun, for assurance…to feel alive despite the contradictory circumstances. What do you want from me here?"

"No." Duncan's cool demeanour wavered only slightly. "Don't dodge this Edgar. That's exactly the question you need to be asking yourself right now."

"Well, I certainly wasn't looking for a damn crush from 14 years ago. I wasn't looking for that!" Edgar's voice trembled as he spoke. He tipped his flask high and held it there a long time.

"What then? Angels? More booze? I don't believe that Eds, even if you do. Fourteen years ago or not, you were happy with her. You had at least some semblance of direction then. You're constantly talking about how things will always work out if you believe, but they haven't, have they? Even up here, you've been running through the same bullshit hamster-wheel you have since we first left home. It's not enough. There comes a point when you've got to get off your ass and work for it."

The seismic movements of Duncan's mounting frustration could be felt through the snug interior of the car. Yet still, he remained composed, his steady gaze focused straight ahead.

Infuriating fucking idiot. Edgar hated knowing that Duncan was at least partially right.

"You don't know what you're talking about." It wasn't that he missed Bev, per se. At times, he could hardly even recall her. Still, there was something missing.

Why the hell can't I just be happy in heaven?

Duncan glanced quickly over at his friend, a telling expression on his face. "Edgar, I'll do the driving if I must, but you have got to decide where we're going."

The near-empty flask left Edgar's hand before he was aware of the action; crashing against the dashboard and clattering to the floor. Sticky brown trails of whiskey ran slowly after it.

"What the fuck is wrong with you Duncan? Can't you just give me a break? Christ! This is my damn heaven, and you need to get the hell out!"

Edgar waited, expecting Duncan's smooth, patient voice to return with some self-assured platitude. It didn't come.

I don't know where I'm going, Edgar reflected, *I don't even know how I got to this place. I'm here, I'm dead, and not a single fucking thing has changed.*

Turning testily to push the confrontation, he was immediately dismayed to find Duncan absent. The unmanned wheel jockeyed aimlessly from side to side, and through the windshield, the horizon began to veer.

Edgar panicked, grasping desperately for the wheel. Catching it, he pulled—too hard in his drunken state—jarring it sharply to the right. The fields became blurs of green and the sky a daze of blue as the car jumped the embankment and took to the air.

Time froze, and in the back of his reeling mind, Edgar heard a familiar refrain: "Where are you going, Edgar?"

But time has little patience, and as the question echoed in his mind, he watched the car's nose turn downward. The ground was coming fast and Edgar knew he was powerless to prevent the impact.

CHAPTER 6
THE IMPLACABLE INQUISITION

There had always existed countless anti-social descriptors that could have been—and on many occasions had been—fairly leveled at Edgar Vincent. Callous and egocentric, he'd had more drinks thrown in his face than most men ever had occasion to imbibe. He'd been slapped enough times for a monolithic highlight reel, and more justifiably-offended men had attacked him in defense of their slighted ladies than even Edgar could count.

He'd caused the premature ending of countless parties and had inadvertently, according to him, led to the permanent shutting down of more than a few bars. He'd facilitated the destruction of more marriages than the combined forces of money and children, and, if rumour could be trusted, may have even contributed to the excommunication of a minister.

Nevertheless, in many an impassioned and inevitably intoxicated rant, Edgar was adamant about his intrinsic talent, despite all contrary evidence, for bringing people together.

It wasn't an entirely baseless claim; however, there was no doubt that this particular proclivity of Edgar's had a tendency to play out with—unexpected results.

On one occasion, which Edgar was fond of relating, he'd invited a new lady friend over to his abode. Never one to discourage the growth of social potential, he'd taken the further initiative of encouraging her to "bring some friends."

Later, when she had arrived with her elderly but enthusiastic parents in tow, Edgar finally found cause to question the ambiguity of his phrasing.

"I'm just an old-fashioned sort of girl, you know," she'd explained with a gleeful giggle.

"I did not know," Edgar corrected flatly.

Still, the wine had already been opened and the oysters set, so he'd hit play on the Marvin Gaye CD he had queued, and brazenly proceeded with one of the most awkward and frequently recounted meals of his life.

Edgar had an especially impressive ability to unite women unknown to one another in their sudden and passionate distaste for his apparently shared company; and he often claimed the legendary success of his late-night endeavours had likely spawned at least one support group for cuckolded men.

In fact, it was this very talent for bringing people together that Edgar aimed to utilize even as he stumbled through the dark drifts of fog all around him.

This mysterious fog effect is getting awfully tiring, he noted.

He moved with slow, careful steps, searching desperately for direction as he tried to focus his throbbing mind on the object of his desire.

Did it always have this shitty rotten-egg smell to it? he wondered. His palms passed defensively along the worn and ragged sleeves of his jacket. *Heaven is over-rated. They really need to get their act together.*

Edgar harboured no recollection of escaping the car. He remembered his argument with Duncan and the long, empty stretches of highway so eager to lead them nowhere. He could recall the car leaving the road and bracing himself for impact. Then he was here, and terribly hung-over.

I should be thankful I made it out alive, but then again… He allowed himself not even the slightest chuckle at this grim observation.

The realization that his hangover had again been renewed was a continuing source of tremendous frustration. His eyes felt like orbs of sand in the snare-drum confines of his aching skull.

In spite of all this, Edgar now at least had no doubt about his intentions. *Due time I get to the bottom of this whole absurd affair,* he determined.

Surprisingly, death had done little to dampen his overall spirits. The strange fact that he'd somehow ended up in heaven, he could get over. Even the understanding that "heaven" consisted primarily of the trying cycle of visiting and revisiting the scattered concerns of his now-ended life was something he could live with.

It even has a certain familiarity to it, he admitted.

What Edgar could not abide, however, was the notion that the timeless tale, which had been The Life and Times of Edgar Vincent, could possibly have ended in any way unbefitting its admirable legacy.

It all came together in an intricate little riddle.

Having woken up in heaven, Edgar could only assume his final moments must have represented some of the noblest and most selfless acts of his entire life.

Admission ain't free, even if the exhibit isn't quite as advertised, he reasoned.

Even ignoring that particular anomaly, Edgar felt fully justified pursuing the details of his tragically untimely ending.

If heaven amounts to little more than an endless foray through my own memories, it stands to reason the route to fulfillment will begin with the event that brought me here, he concluded.

And so, as he continued his lurching shuffle through the viscous and newly reeking fog, Edgar was determined to marshal his resources in a grand effort to ascertain answers. Given the circumstances, this, of course, meant it was once again time for him to bring people together.

With a final halting step, he pushed through the cloying fringes of the fog and walked into the flickering neon light of the Promised Land.

Pulling his jacket up snugly about his neck, he gave a satisfied sigh. The jacket reached just to his waist. Beneath it was a plain, unadorned white undershirt. Along with a pair of blue jeans, Edgar had always liked the way the trim brown coat almost mimicked a suit-jacket to an undiscerning eye, creating that illusory blend of formality and grunge he so adored.

The sign for The Scholar's Lament hummed as he passed beneath it, and the pensive creak of the old wooden door reverberated through his mind with the uncertain echo of half-recalled childhood events.

Through the door, the bar's interior opened up to him with the familiar promise of a drunken debutante. Inside, he was pleased to find the very company he'd counted on, yet startled to discover the details of the locale somewhat at odds with his nostalgic expectations.

The low-ceilinged room wasn't dim in the way he remembered. It was closer to dark. An inky blackness embraced the patrons like so many cloaked predators; while the jarring fluorescent glow from signs along the walls served as the room's sole illumination. This painted the familiar faces inside with alarming shades of circus-clown greens and blues, oranges and reds.

So much fucking red, he grimaced.

The first eyes he met were Tyra's. Leaning up against the dilapidated old popcorn machine, she was busy tonguing an obscenely large lollipop Edgar could only assume was peach flavoured. The machine, for all evidence, was having a harder time of the afterlife than even Edgar. Dinted and lopsided, it stood barely erect amidst a pile of cast-off paint chips and discarded paneling. Smears of age-old grease lined its rusted innards.

To her right, Chanel sat alone at a worn old table. The books formerly serving as ambiance were scattered all about as she pored tirelessly over their torn and cracking pages. Their lizard-skin covers reflected the circus lights off varying shades of brown and olive as the ancient speakers hissed their barely recognizable tunes like the phantom calls of a derelict calliope organ.

A delicate, haunting wail accompanied the struggling speakers, rising and falling with the tinny sounds in a not-quite-melodic facsimile of the tune. Turning to trace the sound, he located Tiffany. Her energetic yellow and white polka-dot dress whirled around her lithe figure as she danced precariously upon one of The Scholar's flimsy roundtables.

Surrounding her, a group of unfamiliar angels howled and swayed, encouraging her histrionic display. The table's base vacillated with each step as Tiffany teetered on the edge of disaster.

Just beyond them sat the titular scholar, cutting a nearly familiar pose within the sickening approximation of the bar that had formerly been amongst Edgar's fondest memories.

The quasi-man sat with the toilsome patience he'd always demonstrated, his worn posture curling him over the dirty wooden tabletop like a punch to the gut.

The original paint was all but gone, revealing the bland grey of its ceramic structure beneath. More than ever before, the years of graffiti and vandalism wore heavily upon his defeated countenance. His eyes were painted over in yellow and red, and his speculative frown was scratched and clawed into the jagged semblance of a madman's grin. Across his narrow chest, as if to leave no doubt whatsoever about his situation, was scrawled a broad, imposing, Fuck.

Some details appeared impervious to change, however. Across the frail shoulders of the pitiable scholar lay the heavy, thick-veined arm of Jake. He sat slouched over the table, his eyes glassy as a discoloured line of saliva ran down the stubbled edge of his square jaw.

They were all there in fact, exactly as Edgar had intended.

Alex held down his customary spot at the far right of the table, absently twirling his usual glass of red wine between thin fingers. Beside him sat Emeric, his back turned to the door as he stretched his left arm affectionately around the empty seat held for Edgar.

Between Jake and Alex, Duncan's seat sat empty. This brought a satisfied sneer to Edgar's lips. *Just try to dictate my afterlife, will he?*

Surrounding the inner circle's de facto spot, the traditional assortment of enthusiastic freshman and crusty old barflies proved conspicuously absent, affording a sight which instantly turned Edgar's sly grin into a brilliant smile and put the bounce back into his step as he crossed the final stretch of floor towards his vacant seat.

The entire ring of tables around them was loaded to capacity with sparkling crystal glasses. Each table held a different offering, eagerly signaling to Edgar with their own enticing shimmers of bronzes, browns and golds.

After only a moment's consideration, he reached down to select from the table whose intoxicating aroma assured him it contained the remedy to his hung-over state. *Oh, Brandy, I can always count on you,* he fondly acknowledged.

With a quick sip, Edgar backtracked to a table just behind him and helped himself to a shot glass brimming with dark liquor. Even as the glass rose from the table, the dull rumble of the bar fell silent; the final rasp of a long death-rattle.

All eyes turned to Edgar.

"Ladies and gentlemen." Edgar had always considered himself a man with an acute talent for capturing a moment and making it his own; and considering this was nothing if not his moment, Edgar felt he would be remiss not to seize upon the opportunity to elucidate his intentions.

"Thanks for coming out tonight," he continued, straightening his back as he stole a quick hit of brandy before holding the shot glass pointedly out at eye level.

"I realize of course that you didn't have much choice. You're here for one simple reason. Together, I believe we can set to rights the glaring omission of certain facts necessary for my eternal contentment. That's a pretty noble goal, I'm sure you'll all agree."

Jake stared at Edgar with uncomprehending eyes. This was a good sign. The expression of exceptional pride and respect smeared across Emeric's wide face, however, gave Edgar cause for concern. *I must sound like a pretentious douche if that nitwit is enjoying this,* he thought.

"I've been blessed," he announced, now raising his shot glass high. The gesture was promptly mirrored by the bar's myriad population of beautiful and familiar faces, as was his follow-up pounding of the drink and selection of a replacement. Jake slammed his ham-like fists enthusiastically on the table, causing his beer to topple over into his lap and sending Alex into a high-pitched fit of giggles.

"I've been blessed..." Edgar continued, expertly recapping as he waited for the ruckus to subside and the undivided attention of his audience to return to him, "with a unique (in my experience)..." he cast an acknowledging nod over to Alex, "opportunity.

"Here I've found myself, in this rather obtuse realization of heaven. I can see my friends, I can choose my location. For once, I seem to have absolute control over my life. This does come—an admittedly ironic downside—at the cost of my life having recently ended."

A sympathetic 'ahh' passed through the ring of angels now encircling Edgar. Jake rolled his eyes, Emeric shook his head, and Alex gazed suspiciously at his purple-tinted reflection at the bottom of his cup.

"No need for sorrow." Edgar's voice was measured and confident, with just the right touch of humility to counterbalance the singularly self-centered nature of his speech. "My life, it cannot be argued, was an Odyssian epic, and I have few regrets. I have lived well, laughed much, and loved—exceptionally." This sent a pitched squeal of enthusiasm through the cluster of angels. Tyra made a show of nodding revealingly to each of her compatriots in turn. Edgar blushed.

"Yet still…" And here he raised his voice to a passionate crescendo while skillfully drawing and lighting himself a cigarette. He even tossed one instinctually to Alex, who received it with the eager appreciation of a hungry seal. "I have found no peace.

"Despite the boundless opportunity afforded to me by the shaking of my mortal coil, I remain bereft of closure. It's no easy task, I assure you, to set out on a new path while lacking clarity as to the failings of your former attempt.

"I don't know how I died; I've no clue why I'm here. Without this knowledge, it seems hopeless to start anew.

"It is, therefore, my intention, esteemed friends and lovely ladies, to figure out the exact circumstances of my death. I mean to find out just what went wrong, so I can move forward on my path undeterred by doubts from the past. I ask for your cooperation in this, to answer my questions and hear my concerns.

"I am aware, my apparitional amigos, how entirely tethered your limited minds are to my own perceptions, but I hope that together we can explore my shortcomings, resolve my mistakes, and set me on course to wherever I'm headed from here."

Eat your heart out, Duncan, he thought.

"To that end, I offer this toast!" Edgar raised his shot glass, and the uproar of appreciation that answered was a breakwater against the floods of his existential ennui.

With that, he pounded his shot. Not one to play favourites, he did likewise with his brandy, grabbed another drink, scotch this time, and assumed his place amongst his friends.

"Geez, Edgar." It was Emeric who spoke first, "I had no idea you were still so hung up on the cause of your death."

"Yeah," Edgar sighed, "I know it shouldn't seem so important. It doesn't make any real difference now that I'm here. But I can't just let it go. It was my life, after all. The whole time I've been here, I've felt none of the peace you'd expect. I mean, this is heaven, right?"

"If you can't be at peace in heaven," Alex struggled to form the words around the constant stream of smoke-rings emanating from his mouth, "then it's really not much of a heaven at all."

"Exactly!" Edgar pounded the table encouragingly. "How can I just close the book on my life without any resolution?"

From across the table came a snort, and Jake gestured sloppily about the bar. "Your life don't look like it's changed that much, Domingo."

Edgar moaned his derision. For as long as he'd known Jake, the bumbling lummox had been utterly entranced by the fact that Edgar bore a Spanish middle-name. Despite countless conversations on the topic, with Edgar tirelessly explaining that the name had been given in honour of his maternal grandmother, Jake still harboured suspicions that he was shamefully concealing his fluency in Spanish, and on several occasions, had demanded that Edgar present him with his "papers."

"But you're a mental invalid, Jake. What would you know?" Edgar took a long drink of scotch to quell his mounting frustration.

"Yeah, I'm not so sure, Jake," said Emeric, "things have changed for Edgar more than anyone seems to acknowledge."

"Thank you, Dirty Emmy," said Edgar.

Jake began to rise shakily from the table—a certain indication that he was seconds away from clobbering poor Emeric—but was quickly settled by a stern look from Edgar.

"Yeah, he's dead for one thing," Alex chuckled, "and he shares his smokes now!" he finished, casting a pleading gaze in Edgar's direction.

"He's also actively obliterating every old record he'd set for continuous alcohol consumption," Emeric continued boldly, a wary eye fixed on Jake. "I know the health risks are irrelevant now, but maybe you'd have more luck finding closure if you approached it with a clear head, Edgar."

"Where's Duncan anyway?" Jake asked, settling carefully back into his seat.

Edgar paid Jake no mind, but quickly passed another cigarette over to Alex. "Don't give me that shit right now, Emmy, I'm in no mood for it. If you had your potential cut short like I have, you'd probably want some way to cope as well. Hell, it would probably loosen you up a bit."

"Yeah!" Jake bellowed triumphantly as he aimed an unsteady finger at the red-haired man. Alex rolled his head in a long, laborious laugh.

"Besides," Edgar continued, his glass glued to his lips, "one of the few things I'm certain of is that I was blind drunk when I died, so getting back into that headspace can hardly be counter-productive, can it?"

"What else do you remember?" asked Alex.

"A sense of imbalance, uncertainty…"

"So, drunk and dizzy then? Now we're making headway," Alex chided.

"I'm serious, Edgar." Emeric pushed his glasses up the bridge of his nose as he spoke, a sure sign he meant business. "I don't mean to belabour the point, and I know that you've always been a pretty…respectable drinker, but being shit-canned every waking moment is just not you. Where's the balance?"

"It doesn't feel like every day though, Emmy. It's all the same. Every day is Sunday; a raging hangover and a million doubts. What am I supposed to do?"

"Well, typically Sunday is preceded by Saturday. If you want to avoid the hangovers, limiting your consumption is a good start, don't you think? Clear your head, and focus on where you're going."

"Last time you told me to focus, I ended up telling Debra I was ready for a commitment."

Edgar had no shortage of jaded former lovers, but Debra held a special place near the top. After drunkenly misconstruing a lecture from Emeric and Duncan about life and direction, Edgar had gone against his better judgment and committed himself to her. Due in part to Edgar's fear of the especially eccentric woman, the relationship lasted a month and a half before Edgar had indulged his taste for variety during a legendary booze-fest with Jake.

A week of car-keying's, broken windows, and small animals in his mailbox had convinced Edgar that the only commitment necessary was of Debra alone.

"Do you think Debra could have done this to me?"

"Seems like a stretch," said Emeric, "didn't she run off with some rock band?"

Edgar shrugged.

"Well," Emeric had dedicated himself to the issue now, and was not about to let it slide, "what else was going on for you before you died? What were you focused on?"

"Wheee!" A loud cheer from Tiffany drew the table's attention to her location. She'd made her way behind the bar and was busy pouring long streams of expensive liquor in the general direction of a row of glasses, as Leslie worked tirelessly to position them under the wavering stream.

"You know what I was focused on," Edgar continued, striving to ignore the ridiculous scene. "BHI. I was nearly done."

"How many years has it been?" A familiar voice echoed in the back of his skull.

Emeric bit his bottom lip, Alex averted his eyes. Jake moved his lips silently before his eyes expanded into saucers of sudden comprehension. "It's an antonym Emeric!" he hollered, causing the entire population of the bar to turn and face him. "B-H-I, it's his band or some shit," he finished, smiling proudly.

This caused Alex to spit his drink across the table as Edgar buried his face in his palms. "Good job Jake, thank you," said Emeric, trying desperately to appease the brute.

"Well, do you remember who you were with when it happened?" asked Alex.

"I know it wasn't you," Edgar answered.

"Because you're dead," Jake explained, placing a consoling paw on Alex's sloping shoulder.

"Well?" Emeric rejoined.

"Well, I was pretty drunk." Edgar scratched his chin reflectively. "So it probably wasn't you, unless I was nagged to death. And judging by the hangover I woke up with, it couldn't have been a woman either."

The table shared an affirmative nod. In life, Edgar had been a master of monitoring his intake in the presence of potential bedmates.

The eyes of the table all settled on Jake. It took several seconds of confident nods and attempted fist bumps before Jake caught the hidden implication. His first response was to shoot an accusatory glance at the scholar beside him. Realizing the shortcomings of this plan only a few seconds afterward, he turned his attention to the empty chair beside the acquitted scholar. "Where's Duncan?"

"Duncan's unnecessary. Good old Emmy here provides all the doubt and judgment needed for any one man's ethereal paradise." Edgar finished his drink, chucked the glass away behind him, and held his hand out expectantly to the empty air.

With hardly a moments passing, a fresh glass of scotch was placed in his outstretched hand. Taking it, he turned to follow the thin white arm of his salvation to the narrow shoulders, long neck, and scarlet smile of Tyra.

"There you go, baby," she purred, playfully tossing her auburn hair from side to side. "Anything else you…desire?"

"Not unless you can tell me how I died," Edgar answered testily.

"Sorry sweet stuff, but that's a little beyond my realm." The articulate cadence of Tyra's speech seemed entirely out of place as she wavered drunkenly on her high heels. Her mouth gaped wide and welcoming as she gave her lollipop an exaggerated bit of attention. Then, taking the empty seat at the end of the table beside Edgar, she leaned in close, her hot breath teasing his ear as she spoke, "but if you're ready to live again…"

The sight of her by his side made Edgar's blood run cold, and he fought to conceal the shiver crawling up the length of his spine.

"Alright then, smart man," Jake started his challenge before fully swallowing the mouthful of beer which clearly demanded his full attention, sending a long trickle down his chin to mix amid the existing stains on his formerly white wife-beater. "How do you think you died?"

Edgar considered for a moment. "That's what doesn't make sense. Everything was in control. My career was going well, I had a fitting friend for every possible situation…my love life was obviously great."

"And yet death took none of that into account." If Alex's comment was meant to be mocking, the effect was lost entirely in his breathy, speculative tone.

Either way, Edgar took no notice. "I seldom get so blackout drunk beyond the company of you louts, and these days it's rare that we all get to hang out together—present circumstances notwithstanding. So, the question becomes," he continued, puffing on his cigarette like a drunken iteration of Sherlock Holmes, "what could have gone wrong with one of you, to result in my death?"

Emeric and Alex gaped incredulously as Edgar spoke. Jake finished yet another beer, belched, and shared his theory with the table. "I'll bet you anything Emeric killed you."

Edgar laughed. "Well, that's one possibility. Dirty Emmy was always the shady sort, if not quite homicidal. But if it was you I was out with Jake, the cause couldn't be more obvious."

It's actually a wonder he didn't get me killed years ago, Edgar admitted to himself.

The rest of his friends had begun to age and slow down as their tenure at university ran its course, but the younger man had always managed to keep pace with Edgar's more Dionysian proclivities.

"Remember our little 'business trip' to LA?" Edgar prompted with a nostalgic chuckle.

"Our bold business adventure? Oh, I remember…parts of it at least." Jake beamed with pride at his inclusion. He struggled, however, to find the relevance. "Why?"

Edgar laughed, "I was lucky to survive that weekend. Who knows what we might have gotten up to if I was out with you on my last night?"

In point of fact, they had both gotten off easy that weekend.

"What trip to LA?" asked Alex. Death, as Edgar was dolefully learning, left him quite out of the loop.

"Oh yeah." Jake swung his thick arm off the scholar's shoulder and leaned forward to regale the group with his most delicious story. "We went to LA once, just me and Edgar. We got totally wasted!"

After a respectful pause, the table realized that the story, in Jake's mind, had been told to the fullest.

"So, what happened?" Tyra broke the silence, leaning towards Edgar as her eager eyes traced the muscular contours of his body.

Forget hedonistic failings, it's amazing that Jake has remembered to breathe for as long as he has, thought Edgar.

"Well," he was happy enough to take up the tale, "it was all pretty last minute, and we didn't have time to book anything besides the plane. So, I had some business cards printed up at the shop before we left, and we caught our flight with nothing but the clothes on our backs, our tickets, a camcorder, and a pocketful of these business cards."

"Business cards?" Tyra asked around the long straw connecting her lips to her cherry-rimmed glass.

Emeric shook his head and fixed his eyes on the scarred surface of the table.

"Domingo Media Division," Edgar beamed. "We posed as casting agents!"

"Lucky people didn't think we were some fucking foreign news crew," Jake mumbled around the lip of a fresh mug.

"I maintain that Jake'z Bitchez would have been far less effective."

"Effective?" Tyra asked, pointedly adjusting her ample bosom in her less than ample top.

"Yes, effective." Edgar adored few things so much as relating stories of his hijinks. None perhaps, beyond their actual creation. "We spent all our funds renting out a little closet to call our office, then hit up the Hollywood clubs. We told all the burgeoning starlets we were casting for an upcoming film and invited a select handful each night back to our 'office' for 'open auditions.'"

"You should have seen some of these broads," declared Jake. In an attempt to help the table grasp his meaning, he pressed his palms flat against his chest. Then, "Vavoom!" he shouted, pushing his arms out in a wide arc, which managed to send the entire contents of the table spilling all over Tyra and Alex.

Tyra screeched, her layered makeup running down her face as if the booze were water to her witch. Alex moaned, staring forlornly at his now soggy cigarette. He cast a needy gaze over at Edgar as Tyra scampered off into the neon-lit corners of the bar to fix herself up.

I could sit here the rest of eternity and not even scratch the surface of all the potential ways this moron could have gotten me killed, Edgar realized.

"Stop looking to everyone else for your answers Edgar, it's unbecoming of you." The voice was Duncan's, creeping again into Edgar's mind. He shuddered.

Taking a moment to clear his head, Edgar passed yet another smoke to Alex as he lit one for himself. Glancing down, he gawked at the gaping black void in his packet. *Has it grown?* he wondered.

"Anyway," Edgar continued once the table had settled down and the drinks had been replaced. "Needless to say, we didn't pay for a single drink the entire weekend and managed to return with a video that made old Emmy's face match his hair!"

The friends—save poor Emeric—shared a great laugh at this. Edgar had since maintained that Jake also returned with an itch for a special new prescription shampoo, but Jake had never caught the implication, and thus the story remained unsubstantiated.

Jake nodded and smiled, soaking up the laughs like the adulation of an adoring crowd. Edgar had always held that Jake was among the most excessive and dangerously reckless people he'd ever known.

Helpless to the point of handicapped, he reflected. Still, Jake's unflinching loyalty to those who could tolerate him, combined with his borderline hero-worship of Edgar, made it hard to believe he'd allow his friend to die on his watch.

"Of course, as hazardous as Jake can be, Emeric is by far the more insidious danger," Edgar declared with a provocative smirk.

"Now Edgar, don't talk like that," Emeric spoke in a pleading tone, taking a sheepish sip from his new rum and coke.

"And he's the only guy I know with his own Chinese beef dish named after him," Jake grinned as he spoke.

Alex doubled over the table, slapping the back of the over-tolerant and under-maintained scholar, and lost himself in a fit of giggles through which he barely managed to articulate his appreciation. "It's true...ginger beef!"

"Don't be so defensive, Emmy. If we're going to get to the bottom of my death—and we are—we need to consider all the possibilities. And you are, as we all know, the very reason for my ongoing love of spirits."

"Like a barstool evangelist," said Alex listlessly, his pinprick pupils focused on the orange ember of his cigarette.

"It's true." Edgar raised his glass to Emeric, drained it, and placed it in front of his blushing friend. "I was a full month off the sauce when I made the mistake of visiting Emeric at his lovely family home."

"Now that's not fair. You know I didn't have anything to do with..."

"Quiet Emmy, you're being rude. Jake didn't deny the inherent risks he places on those in his company, and neither should you."

Jake leaned back in his chair, interlacing his hands behind his head, proudly, while wearing a shining, shit-eating grin.

Emeric just shook his head silently, picking at a dry stain on the table.

"So, I went over to visit my dear friend and his lovely wife..."

"Yeah," Jake interjected, "she's real..."

"Enough!" Emeric shouted, glaring across the table at the bulky buffoon.

Alex continued to chuckle like a hyena on laughing gas.

Jake moved again to rise, caught an authoritative glare from Edgar, and resumed his seat quietly. While Edgar had always reveled in the borderline abuse of Emeric, he viewed his friend like a harmless little brother and seldom allowed anyone else to mess with him. Along with this "protection", Emeric was afforded an open ticket to some of the most interesting and outrageous scenes he could ever hope to imagine, but could never access alone. Admittedly, and much to Edgar's chagrin, these perceived benefits had begun to diminish once school had ended and Emeric turned his ambitions to more adult pursuits.

How will these dysfunctional idiots ever carry on without me? Edgar mused.

"The question here is more how you're going to carry on, Edgar." It was Duncan's voice again—bleeding into his brain like the ethereal result of some mad moral osmosis. Edgar shook his head and took a long swallow of scotch before proceeding.

"So, I thought I'd visit my dear friend, maybe chat about old times, maybe share a few sentimental stories, perhaps even a few laughs. But that sure wasn't old Emeric's plan. No," he continued, "Emeric felt it would be better to bore me into catatonia. The rat bastard took in a sober man, and inside of an hour, dragged me kicking and screaming right off the wagon."

It was at least partially true. When Edgar had shown up to meet his friend, the mood of the get-together leaned distinctly more towards Emeric's tastes. "A straight hour of nagging and boredom: 'Look at my pretty new duvet.' 'Don't you want to settle down with a nice woman?' 'Do you notice the hint of chamomile in the tea?' 'Have you ever considered relocating to a more family-friendly neighbourhood?' I swear he wouldn't have been happy short of me dying my hair red and developing a penchant for tweed jackets."

"But it wasn't really the boredom that bothered you, was it, Edgar?" Edgar's hands clenched beneath the table, and his head quivered with rage at the grating intrusions of his absent friend.

Edgar had always considered himself an unwavering rebel, a man simply born to live faster and harder than other men. He'd always known his natural talents and charisma were destined to bring him both adoration and fame, but it had taken a bit longer for him to perceive how they also ensured his lifelong independence.

It's not that those things aren't enticing: a wife, a family…a bit of peace now and again, he admitted. *It's just…*

"All that other stuff will come in due time," he'd once told Duncan.

"So, what happened?" asked Alex.

"Well," Edgar shook himself from his reverie to answer. "Once Emeric saw that he'd sufficiently broken my spirit, he directed me straight back onto my road of ruin."

"You broke into my cabinet and stole a 50-year-old bottle of champagne. My mother gave it to me at my wedding!"

Edgar shrugged his complacent agreement. "I also left a fresh stain on your new carpet for good measure, if I recall correctly."

"You do." Emeric frowned, his sad face illuminated in alternating colours by the flashing neon lights of the bar.

Edgar knew he was often too hard on Emeric. It bothered him more than he cared to admit that Emeric had so easily managed to accomplish all of his goals. Even greater was his annoyance when Emmy presumed to offer him advice on his own life; as if the two could ever be compared.

Still, he had trouble convincing himself that Emeric would ever be party to anything that might truly hurt him. *The poor bastard really is harmless,* he accepted.

"Emeric just never understood that I was working towards those things, even if my path was occasionally somewhat—meandering," Edgar spoke as if to himself.

"I only wanted what's best for you, Edgar. You must know that. I just worry about your priorities sometimes," Emeric encouraged, wringing his hands above his diminishing highball glass.

"Where's Duncan?" Alex wondered aloud.

"I threw him out," Edgar answered, his back sliding slowly down his chair as he sipped on his drink and listened nervously for Duncan's invasive voice to press the issue. "He was giving me a hard time about Bev." He cast a sidelong glance at the freshly vacated chair beside him.

"Who the fuck is Bev?" Jake asked.

"No one," Edgar blurted before anyone else could interject. "It's not important. I just wish there was some way to figure out how all this happened."

"Edgar," Emeric placed a delicate hand on his friend's shoulder as he spoke. "Don't you think we've already got a pretty clear picture of what led to your death?"

"What are you saying exactly?" Edgar turned to face his mousey friend, shrugging the hand off his shoulder as he did so.

Emeric's mouth hung open a minute, and his lip trembled as he gazed back into Edgar's stern face. Then his eyes turned downward, and his head sank.

"He's saying it's your own fault—that you need to stop blaming everyone else," Duncan's voice played through his mind, and Edgar looked feverishly about the bar in a fruitless attempt to locate the sanctimonious specter.

"Get out of my head," he grumbled. Around the table, his friends answered only with quizzical stares. Emeric slid his chair back slightly.

"That's it, I'm going out for a toke," said Alex, excusing himself from the table and slipping out the front door.

"Just listen to the stories you're telling Edgar, think about your choices," the haughty bastard in his head was on a tear now and didn't seem ready to stop.

"Hell Edgar, look around you! You can do, go, see anything—anyone you want. You can explore your entire life, revisit your past—and what have you done? You've surrounded yourself with an endless ocean of alcohol and wallowed in your own misery."

"And here I thought I'd surrounded myself with friends." Edgar's voice was venomous.

Emeric swallowed nervously, rattling the melting ice-cubes in his empty cup.

"You're such an asshole Emer-prick," Jake slurred, his bulky frame slowly folding over the rough wooden table under the crippling weight of his inebriation.

Edgar finished his drink and shook his head.

His body still rigid with tension, Emeric leaned in somewhat, his eyes searching Edgar's. "C'mon Edgar, just tell me what you need."

Edgar needed friends and comfort. He needed time and understanding. He needed some indication that despite all evidence to the contrary, things would be alright.

"You need to stop lying to yourself, Edgar," Duncan's even, confident tone came softly, just for Edgar.

"I need a fucking exorcism!" Edgar screamed.

Without thinking, he flipped the table over in a fury, scattering his remaining friends and the surrounding angels.

Struggling out of his seat, Edgar stumbled, sending his chair tumbling over backwards. He wheeled his hands around frantically, catching the edge of the table behind him as he fell.

His back hit the ground hard, knocking the wind from his lungs as the table, still held firmly in his grasp, tipped on its base, bringing glass after glass of brandy tumbling down over him.

It came as a tempest; an unceasing shower of the pungent bronze liquor staining his shirt, soaking his jacket, and burning his eyes. It spread out all around him, dark and fragrant as he lay still on the hard, damp floor.

All was quiet.

Dead quiet.

Edgar opened his eyes, and above him shone the stars; cold and uncaring. The silence was all-consuming. The bar was gone. The angels were gone. His friends were gone.

He remembered the night of his death; the dizziness, the uncertainty. He recalled again the strange motivation to push onward, the doubt as to where he would end up. Again, he could see the tall, foreboding building looming just out of reach. Lying on his back, he felt once more the sudden surge of terror, the maddening thrill as his desperately precarious sense of balance had failed him.

He looked around: one side, then the other. Nothing answered his gaze but the murky fog of the unknown and the infinitely patient stars above. Sitting up slowly, he marshaled his focus on the faint echoes of the night he'd died.

I was alone, he knew.

"They never tell you how lonely it is, do they?" The hoarse voice, punctuated by a series of rough coughs, belonged to Alex. He stood next to Edgar now, the two of them lost together in the void. A long, hand-rolled joint hung fuming between his lips.

"They tried," Edgar groaned, rising from the puddle of brandy still spreading across the empty, ethereal planes of his afterlife.

Alex grimaced, but offered no response.

Taking the joint from his friend, Edgar pulled on it long and hard, promptly erupting into a violent coughing fit. "Still getting the good shit up here, I see. So, how is everyone doing down there, anyway? In real life, I mean."

"Well," replied Alex, "how do you imagine they're doing?"

"We both know that's all that's really happening here," Edgar answered, taking a second puff before passing the joint back to Alex. "So skip the niceties and make with my speculations."

"They miss you, Edgar."

Edgar nodded, crushing his eyelids together tightly to deny the truth. He had nothing to say.

"You know," Alex broke the silence, his goofy face wreathed in a thick billow of smoke, "you told stories about everyone at the table…everyone but me."

Edgar shook his head, "It's not like that Alex, buddy. It's just that I knew it couldn't have been your fault. You couldn't have been there. You're…"

"Story is over," Alex interjected.

"Yeah," said Edgar, accepting the smoke back from his old pal, "and so is mine."

The two friends stood silently for a long while, sharing the joint and watching the smoke drift indifferently off to blend with the endless, all-encompassing fog that enveloped them.

It was Alex who finally spoke, "You know, Duncan wasn't wrong."

Edgar did a double take, his mind racing to conceive how Alex could know about the disembodied voice. A quick consideration of the circumstances rendered the question irrelevant, however. "I know." Edgar's powerful voice came frail in the vastness of the void. "I just can't deal with all that right now."

"Not about the lies. Well, them too, but that's not what I meant. I mean about what you're doing here. What you could do."

Edgar arched an inquisitive eyebrow at his friend, but maintained his silence.

"You can do anything you want now. Your entire existence is limited only by your own imagination. Why not use that to its full potential? I mean, really take advantage of what blessings remain and get to the bottom of things; find or create some way to get what you need?"

Edgar drew deeply from the joint, holding the burning smoke in his lungs and feeling his head swim. *My story may be over,* he reflected, *but it does deserve a final, proper screening.*

"You know what, pal?" Edgar spoke slowly, his thoughts already far away. Pursing his lips together in the middle, he exhaled through the corners of his mouth, sending long blades of smoke slicing high up into the air at each side of his head. "You may be on to something."

Edgar smiled, and without another word, walked off into the darkening wall of fog.

CHAPTER 7
THE INFERNAL SHIT-SHOW

In life, Edgar Vincent had been a bastard. No one could really deny it. Few had ever tried. When confronted with the consequences of his invariably self-serving actions, even Edgar could do little more than shrug his shoulders and misrepresent the facts.

Certainly, there had been moments when he would offer some hint of protest: cursing fate and decrying how circumstances had conspired against him. For instance, when Edgar had managed to convince his new friend Emeric to join him for a night of "casual drinks," he'd sworn on everything sacred to make it his sole purpose to keep the less experienced boy safe and out of trouble.

The following day, he had explained to a bloody, battered, and freshly shaven Emeric that he was entirely blameless. How was he to know that Emeric would handle his liquor so poorly?

Emeric was never fully convinced that excuse held water. Edgar had since decided that wasn't his fault either.

On a more recent occasion, upon realizing a lady he'd been seeing casually, Celeste, had managed to develop feelings for him despite his fervent efforts to prevent this very occurrence, Edgar took it upon himself to let her down with as little conflict and heartache as humanly possible.

He'd arranged to meet her at her favourite spot in the City Park, then shut off his phone and went out with Jake. Celeste, he reasoned, would figure out that he wasn't coming, and accept her misjudgment alone, free of embarrassment in the calming comfort of nature.

But Edgar wasn't a goddamn meteorologist and had no knowledge of the impending thunderstorm. So when he'd later learned that Celeste had been admitted to the hospital with hypothermia, he felt the fault was at least not entirely his own. He'd sent a bouquet of white roses with a Friends Forever card, and chalked it up to lessons learned.

Still, no matter the trouble that surrounded him or the lectures he received, Edgar always remained steadfast that in all of his choices, and behind each of his misadventures, he had only the best of intentions. *But I can't imagine good intentions are enough for admittance to a place like this,* he thought.

They weren't.

Edgar had left Alex after the incident at The Scholar with a fresh new perspective on the potential of his afterlife. If his reality was truly the product of his own expectations, he intended to finally use that knowledge to figure out this whole confounding affair once and for all.

Of all the god-forsaken, awkward bastards walking that earth, how could I have managed to die alone? he wondered, walking again through the murky fog for what seemed like an eternity. His death was a mystery surpassed only by his miraculous admittance to heaven, and if Edgar was going to put those questions to rest, then perhaps it was time for a trip down memory lane.

"Not much of a lane really," said Edgar. Smoke billowed from his mouth with each word.

Indeed, it was not.

When the mist finally dissipated, he stood for a moment rubbing his temples, trying to discern whether his vision was reality or some sickening twist of the senses resulting from his recent heavenly excesses.

In a place like this, he thought with an ironic smirk.

Beneath his feet, a checkerboard marble floor stretched off in all directions. Each square was large enough to stand in, with the full reach of his outstretched arms never passing the edge on any one side. These dichotomous squares extended beyond sight. Over the distance, they seemed to shrink away, until they were like opposing grains of sand rattling off across the terrible expanse, fading again into the fog.

Something about the scene made him squirm.

Pillars reached up at irregular intervals, meandering and bending like the trunks of trees or the truth of a tale that's changed in the telling. Some showed signs of branching, splitting here or there for short stretches. Inevitably, however, one branch would die off or else bend upon its course to rejoin the dominant strand.

Edgar turned slowly on his axis, as much from his earnest desire to take in the stunning panorama as from the overwhelming sense of vertigo accompanying his customary Sunday-morning nausea.

The pillars appeared in deep blacks, and luminous whites, and every shade of grey in between. The hue of some shifted as he focused on them—now darker, now lighter.

Their shapes and branches swayed and changed as well. It was barely noticeable to an intent gaze, yet sufficient in a gestalt effect to reveal to Edgar a scene disconcertingly foreign each time he completed a full rotation, keeping him in a constant state of disorientation. Something about the iridescent pillars reminded Edgar of a diagram he'd seen back in high-school biology, but that course had been especially distracting for the hormonally- charged young man, and his fried neurons could not quite recall what it had represented.

"If this really is a product of my expectations," Edgar spoke aloud; noticing at the base of each pillar a small assortment of glowing shapes, dwarfed by the monolithic structures towering above, "then my expectations are truly fucked."

"Welcome." The voice came from behind him, shattering the eerie silence and nearly causing Edgar to piss his…

"What the fuck is this? A robe?" he demanded, realizing for the first time the strange nature of his garb.

"More of a tunic, really," answered the voice. Turning, Edgar was met with familiar piercing grey eyes and an unnervingly stoic smile.

"Pete." Edgar's eyes narrowed to slits, and his voice dripped with contempt.

"The very same." The man's voice was calm and timeless, and the silver of his hair shone in the ethereal glow of the expansive realm.

"Shut up, Pete. What am I wearing? And where am I?"

"What you're wearing is entirely up to you. As I said, it appears to be a tunic of some sort; maybe a toga. It's quite swaddling, either way. As for where you are, I'd been getting to that, before you interrupted."

"What are you talking about?" Edgar angrily entreated. Then, after a moment's consideration, petulantly added, "And it's not a toga!"

"I'd said," Pete answered with a gentle grin on his face. "Welcome."

Edgar was fuming now, which did little to settle the uneasy tides of his churning stomach. "Well get on with it, Jeeves!"

"Welcome," Pete continued cheerfully, "to the Hall of Memories. And," he added, the faintest hint of testiness creeping into his voice, "don't call me that."

Pete stood tall and proud, watching Edgar with serene patience. He remained utterly still, Edgar noticed—no rise and fall of breath altered his posture, no flutter of eyelids compromised the ancient integrity of his countenance. *Creepy shit*, thought Edgar.

With a mammoth sigh, Edgar surrendered. "So then, what is a man meant to do in the Hall of Memories?"

"May I start you off with a refreshment?" The perfectly sincere cordiality of Pete's voice made Edgar want to throw up. When the enigmatic man stepped aside to reveal a neat little table covered with intricate crystal decanters, follow-through seemed all but assured.

Edgar's hands clenched at his sides, and his guts did sloppy somersaults. His head raged, but staring at the table, he swore again that he heard the singing of angels.

Angel song, however, had recently been proven somewhat less than heavenly by Tiffany's sorry example at The Scholar, and with a determination that surprised even him, Edgar answered, "You know Petey, I think I'll pass."

"As you like," answered the strange man. Edgar thought his tone betrayed a hint of excitement, but then again, he'd just been relieved of bartending duties. "Explore as you wish," Pete continued with a graceful gesture behind his guest, "I'll be available if you should need me."

Goddamn right you will be, thought Edgar.

Turning on his heel to strut away, Edgar was stopped dead in his tracks before he even reached mid-saunter. Looming up directly ahead of him was one of the gargantuan pillars. It throbbed and wavered as he watched, its surface shimmering between hues of light and dark like the intentions of an unchecked and unsatiated ambition.

At the column's base burned a small fire, surrounded by candles and incense sticks sending off sweet aromas. Drawing up before the quaint display, Edgar's nose twitched, sifting through the convoluted potpourri of smells like an experienced archaeologist intent on a hidden relic. Beneath the cinnamons and lilacs and all the other sickly false scents of the burning incense was something strangely familiar.

His attention settled finally upon the central fire as he continued to take quick searching sniffs of the air. It smoldered more than it burned, he noted. A tiny tuft of flame rose from its epicentre, while the peripheries merely glowed in flickering shades of orange and red. The smoke rising from it was a light grey—bordering on white and, as he focused his olfactory senses on the sought-after scent, Edgar felt a wave of nostalgia wash over him.

*****

It was early in Edgar's first year of university. As he followed the promising scent floating on the air out of the bushes and across the small field behind his dormitory tower, he was increasingly certain the night was about to pick up.

Edgar fussed with a fresh scuff on his brown leather jacket as he approached the edge of a gentle incline. There, he found a scrawny young man standing alone in the light of the moon, exactly as he expected.

The boy wore a faded Depeche Mode t-shirt and torn jeans. His shaggy blonde hair—longer and more unkempt than even Edgar had allowed his own to grow in his first hedonistic months of university—swayed along to the tunes Edgar could only assume played through the headphones cupped over his tiny ears.

But none of that interested Edgar. What did interest him was the long, reeking joint dangling loosely from the young man's scruffy mouth.

Walking cheerfully up behind him, Edgar thanked his lucky stars for the fine turn the night had taken. Duncan had gone out with what Edgar could only assume was some haggard troll, which left him to entertain himself. His liquor had quickly run dry, however, and he hadn't yet secured a source of anything more illicit.

"Hey!" Edgar called out, but the gangly boy just continued to puff away, his head bouncing along to unheard melodies.

"Hey," he tried again, gently tapping his saviour on the shoulder this time.

Spinning around gracelessly and loosing an undignified squeal, the young man's eyes grew wide.

Standing with his gorgeous leather jacket hanging carelessly over his tight white undershirt, Edgar smiled. He placed his weight on one leg, a cool expression on his face. His hair was styled with surprising care considering the hour. With the full moon acting as a backlight to his cocky posturing, Edgar shouldn't have been surprised at the question from the blazingly high boy before him.

Nor was he.

"Whoa…are you, like, a rock star?" the boy had asked.

Edgar's effort to conceal his satisfaction paid off, allowing only an arrogant sneer as he sized the boy up, confirming his suspicions. As soon as he'd smelled the pot on the air, Edgar had guessed the source to be Alex, a student from another floor he'd met only a few weeks earlier—under shockingly similar circumstances. Edgar had noted at the time, however, that Alex was an understandably absent-minded sort of guy, and so Edgar was giddy to see how this new encounter would play out.

"Not exactly," he answered with an easy chuckle. "Hey, I don't mean to be the typical first-year pseudo-commie, but would you mind if I got in on that?"

"Oh, oh yeah man. Yeah, by all means," Alex said with an apologetic tone as he handed the doobie over without a second thought.

"Thanks," said Edgar, taking it gratefully. "Hey, what's your name?"

"Oh, uh, Ted," the stranger answered, casting his eyes downward. "I'm Ted."

Edgar snickered to himself. His suspicion that the memory of their first encounter was lost on the fidgety young stoner had now been confirmed. "Well, it's nice to meet you A…Ted."

"You too man, you too."

"I'm Edgar," he offered, smiling happily at the night's direction.

"Oh, Edgar hey? Nice to meet you, Edgar."

"Likewise, Ted," Edgar replied; stealing a third hit before passing the joint back.

"Hey thanks!" exclaimed "Ted"—as if accepting an unexpected gift. Edgar laughed aloud at this, but the disheveled man pushed on undeterred. "So Edgar, if you're not a rock star, what do you do?"

"I'm a student, in fact," Edgar answered, stating the obvious solely for his own amusement, "but I am working to get into the music industry, sort of."

"Oh, very cool," answered Ted. "Wait, what do you mean, sort of."

"Well, I make music, but rock isn't my thing exactly. Lately, I'm more taken by film scoring, to be honest. I really appreciate the power music has to add so exponentially to a moment—in film and life alike," Edgar explained, surprised at how the unassuming nature of the local pothead served to soften Edgar's typically ironic front. The observation didn't bother him, however, and he'd continued on freely.

"I love films, documentaries, really anything with a statement to make. People are so often too scared to speak their mind or be themselves, and that's a terrible thing. If my music can help increase the clarity or impact of some wise words, then I feel like it's important."

"Don't you ever worry you'll never be able to make your own statement?" asked Ted. He stared at the moon, blowing tiny bursts of smoke at it as if expecting a response.

"I really don't think that's true at all. I'll be able to choose my projects carefully, and more often than not good music contributes significantly to any great idea. I mean, pupil-dilation and double-headed dildos are one thing, but what would *Requiem* be without its score? That power—that's all up to me, my friend."

"Oh. So, what is it you really want to say then?" Ted asked.

"I'm coming, motherfuckers!" Edgar grinned as he made the joke—an unabashedly charming gesture well-known for its ability to get under the skin of those who knew no better. "To be honest, there are just so many things I want to say, and so many people trying to say them. My talent is music, so that's how I can contribute. Maybe someday I'll find a project that feels like a direct extension of my own views and passions, or maybe I'll have to write one myself. I don't know, but I'm sure whatever I need to say, I'll find a way, eventually."

The scrawny young man gazed downward, shaking his head sadly. "Hey, you seem like a really cool guy, Edgar. I've gotta be honest with you man. My name's not Ted. It's Alex."

Edgar feigned shock momentarily, but ultimately let the point slide, feeling half-bad about his own deception. "No worries, Alex. You've got to be careful who you trust after all. So, what are you into?" The question was sincere. The other time they'd met, Edgar had learned painfully little about the man, opting instead to bask in Alex's shameless admiration as he shared a few stories of recent sexual dalliances.

"Oh me?" Alex gaped, and Edgar couldn't be certain if it was excitement or bewilderment. "Well, I'm into art, I guess. Any art at all, really. I draw myself—I mean, I don't draw pictures of myself—that would be weird. I just do it, draw you know…but it doesn't really matter. I just want to take it all in; the sights, the tunes, and the stories, I just…want to take it all in," Alex finished conclusively.

"Do you ever," Edgar agreed, gazing towards the joint lingering over-long in the hands of its rightful owner. Accepting it back along with a heartfelt apology, he continued, "I know what you mean, though. If I can spend the rest of my life working with great films and making compelling music"—Alex nodded along—"and continuing to enjoy all the luxuries that come with the lifestyle, then I'll be pretty damn happy, my friend."

Edgar watched Alex's eyes grow wide at his final reference, and his pulse quickened. "You know what I'm talking about, right buddy?" he prompted eagerly.

"Luxuries?" Alex croaked amidst a sudden coughing fit.

Edgar beamed. "Yeah, my man, of course. Wealth, women, and wanton hedonism—they're an artist's birthright after all." Alex stood in a state of visible awe, which of course only encouraged Edgar. With Alex's envious gaze fixed upon him, Edgar felt just as he needed to—alive.

"It's funny," Edgar continued slowly enough to conceal his enthusiasm, "I was actually just upstairs watching TV, when I heard this voice coming down the hall...'Edgar, Edgar,' it called," he said, in a high nasal tone. "'Edgar where are you?' I knew it was this Cassandra girl from last weekend and ended up jumping out the second-floor window to avoid the headache," he finished the more-or-less accurate telling, fussing again with his scuffed jacket.

Alex broke out in a fit of hysterical, high-pitched giggles, small puffs of smoke accompanying each burst. Edgar beamed, holding up just long enough for Alex's barrage to subside—a fair while, as it turned out. When the time came, at last, he continued, "Hell, just yesterday, I was minding my own business, strumming my guitar, when this girl walked into the lounge. Now, I could tell by looking at her that she was an impending disaster. But I tell you, my friend," and here he gave Alex a lascivious look, "no impending disaster had ever looked so good in stilettos."

Alex's eyes turned to saucers, and Edgar's heart raced. With a quick tug on the collar of his jacket, he smiled and continued, "So anyway..."

*****

The small fire continued to flicker in front of him, but the memory was gone. Edgar couldn't recall exactly what story he'd told Alex that night—it blended in with so many other raucous tales he'd shared with his enthusiastic friend in the years since. Alex had always been an eager audience for Edgar's braggadocio.

He thought about Alex, and about what had happened. The little pot-fire with its surrounding collection of candles and incense took new meaning before his eyes: a sudden funeral shrine for a lost friend.

It made for a hell of a second meeting, he reflected sadly, *but we grew past that initial dishonesty.*

Looking back, Edgar assured himself that he'd really meant nothing but the best. Playing up his rebellious nature had been entirely for the entertainment of that wild-eyed stranger. *He needed the excitement. Besides, I was an inspiration to Alex,* he thought. *Someone needed to fill that spacious skull of his.*

Edgar's head sank.

He and Duncan drove out to the scene of the accident the day Alex had died. They'd never discussed why, after all those years apart, Edgar had still been his emergency contact.

But the wreck still lingered in his mind. The hood cut straight down the centre, the tires turned out sideways. He could recall the glare of the sheared metal where the emergency-responders had cut Alex's lifeless body free, and the fucked up feeling in his gut when he'd noticed the faint marijuana scent rising up from the stained upholstery, as if Alex were right there beside them, ready to pass to the left.

Pulling out a smoke and sparking it to life, he dropped the pack back into his pocket. The remaining cigarettes made a faint thumping noise as they jostled around the growing void within.

It's not that I ever really lied to Alex, he consoled himself, but the sinking sensation in his stomach would not retreat. If anything, Edgar had always endeavoured to be a leader, an anchor to the select few he cared about.

Not in the dragging down sense…

Taking a long drag as he tugged self-consciously at the edges of his pristine white tunic, he smiled. Best intentions be damned—his present state was proof enough that fond memories were fundamental, and if nothing else, Edgar was confident he'd helped in forming many of those.

Truth be told, Edgar had always reasoned that there was a deeper level of altruism in even his most deplorable adventures—as his actions provided memories others could not provide themselves.

This line of reasoning had been solid enough for Edgar in life, but just now, he felt the ground was churning beneath him, and he wanted only to put distance between himself and the ghoulish funeral display. Turning abruptly, he passed quickly between pillars along the great checkerboard expanse, hurrying as if to outrun the uneasy feeling growing in his gut.

The pillars all around him continued to sway and shift in colour, but one just ahead stood out amongst the rest. Its base was surrounded by shining objects and bright spots of colour.

Drawing nearer, he determined the source of the shininess to be empty tequila bottles littering the marble floor. The colours, he realized with an excited grin, were a scattering of bikini tops. *Now, this seems like a story worth recalling,* he thought, grinning bravely as he stepped towards the incandescent pillar.

Picking up a tequila bottle, Edgar turned it over in his hand, watching the remainder splash and slosh about in the bottom. *Barely even a sip left,* he observed, *but perhaps that's for the better.*

A clear head is the best thing right now, just like Emeric said. Edgar tossed the bottle down lazily. *I know I did some good down there, at least where my friends are concerned. I need to focus on those times. Everything else will be alright.*

Yet staring down at the scattered bottles and discarded bikini tops, even Edgar doubted the claim was entirely true. He had a queer feeling about the meaning behind the items. Not a suspicion exactly, certainly not a recollection. Yet the thought of tequila just then made his stomach rage in protest, and judging by the strange scene around him, Edgar knew there had to be a damn good reason for that.

*****

"Hurry up, you idiots," Edgar had called out mid-stumble. Immediately afterward, the stumble had matured into a full-on fall, landing poor Edgar flat on his face and shattering the half-empty bottle of tequila in his hand.

"What are we meant to be hurrying, exactly?" Duncan asked. He stood with an air of effortless confidence. His pressed, white-collared shirt was all but covered by a clean, black pea coat.

"Helping me," Edgar answered as he struggled to his feet and moodily examined a new scuff on the elbow of his beloved leather jacket. "We have to pull this off perfectly, or this deplorable creep will never forgive us." His words came in a staccato stutter of faux-sincere hysteria as he gestured in the direction of a young and utterly humiliated Emeric.

"Bring me that bucket!" Edgar demanded of no one in particular. No one responded. "And where the fuck is Alex?"

"You only sent him off half an hour ago." Duncan defended their absent friend.

"Yeah, and he's probably been lost for twenty minutes already. C'mon everybody." With this, Edgar spun around to face Emeric and held his hands skyward in a dramatically hollow gesture. "This son-of-a-bitch managed to meet some actual women tonight, despite all the odds against him. I'll be god-damned if we can't make a worthy memory of it for him."

"And you are absolutely certain both of these things are necessary to achieve that?" asked Duncan, holding up a pair of rubber boots and an entire case of Jello mixture.

A chorus of nervous laughter rose from a ring of five bikini-clad women swaying drunkenly and shivering under a blanket next to Emeric, whose already red face only darkened. Emeric sighed—a long cloud billowing into the brisk December air—but his eyes remained glued to the ground.

Dropping a partially inflated rubber duck inner-tube, Edgar stumbled over to his infinitely more lucid friend, and pushed a quivering finger into Duncan's unimpressed face. "Yes Duncan, I am actually. Look at him." Here, Edgar wheeled his accusing finger over toward Emeric. "Do you really think he's ever done anything really fun? I mean, really, crazy fun?" Edgar had no time to wait for a response. "No!" he testified like a late night televangelist, "he hasn't. And you're not going to stop me from changing that."

"Edgar, you're being ridiculous. The poor, awkward mope hates this, and you need to stop." Bev interjected from just beside Duncan. She wore tight jeans, which complemented her curvy hips, and a thin black leather jacket over a loose-fitting Led Zepplin shirt, which lent an unspoken modesty to her humbly pretty face.

Edgar turned to face her, his frenzied demeanour momentarily subsiding. "Bev," Edgar groped for words, the artifice of his charismatic confidence cast asunder by the expectant glow of her round face. "Baby," he finally continued, gesturing between himself and Emeric as he did, "there are only two ways to live."

Edgar dashed off in search of one of the many other bottles of tequila he'd purchased on off-sales. Emeric sidled casually up to Bev, his eyes still locked on the snow-laden earth beneath them. "Sorry about all this," he mumbled.

The apology was entirely unjustified on Emeric's part. He'd only met Edgar a few weeks prior, in fact, and despite being halfway through their first year of university, that meeting had been his first night of significant indulgence. The day after, Emeric ran a trembling hand over the bright red stubble of his itching scalp and swore to avoid the deviant charmer forevermore.

"Oh," Bev spoke with the gentle grace of a woman beyond her years. "I'm quite certain none of this was your fault."

Having known Edgar quite intimately since the first month of the school year, and being his devoted partner for very nearly four months now, there was no question Bev was correct. In fact, Edgar had openly struggled since that fateful first night out to continue taking advantage of Emeric's naïve nature. "Show him the ways of the world," he'd called it.

This night, Emeric had finally given in once again. It went to hell in no time. The two men, under the strict guidance of Edgar, had quickly connected with a contingent of ladies from the school's volleyball team. Edgar had immediately asked them several intricate yet ambiguously worded questions about "bumping" and then proceeded to forget about Emeric entirely for the next several hours.

The tequila had flowed, and as the red-faced Emeric stared blankly at the table, he'd heard the conversation turn from volleyball, to beach volleyball, to bikinis, to the absence of bikinis.

Then it kept going until Emeric had finally been dragged unceremoniously out the door by Edgar, who rapidly phoned friends and made grandiose claims about the night's potential.

They stood now in a small park just off campus, with an illegal bonfire warding off the season's chill as Edgar struggled to back up his wild assertions.

"Hey, where did you put that ladle?" he called into the still night air. This elicited a loud laugh from Duncan, an exasperated sigh from Bev, and a passing of nervous glances between the increasingly doubtful group of volleyball players.

Bev slipped away from the group, motioning for Edgar to follow as she moved out of the fire's light into the blackness of the park beyond. "Edgar, what are you doing here? You've got all this useless shit, you've sent poor Alex off to get god knows what, these damn girls are utterly confused if not somewhat let down...dammit Edgar! 'Utterly' is not a funny word!" she cut her point short as Edgar slipped off into a fit of laughter.

"No, no. It's not that Bev. Although it absolutely is a funny word. It's just, I just realized his name sort of rhymes with limerick...I have to use that some time." Edgar went to pass a hand casually through the long tuft of uncombed hair jutting out from the back of his ball cap, missed entirely, and promptly gave up the endeavour.

"Edgar, Jesus..." said Bev, wavering on her heel as she debated simply walking away right then. "Emeric's a nice enough guy, why do you have to fuck with him so much?" she asked, placing a gentle hand on Edgar's shoulder before she finished, "...to say nothing of me."

"Bev," Edgar slurred, missing her addendum entirely. "I'm not fucking with him. I'm helping him. How many memories will he have the way he's living? Come on, life will pass him by with all the excitement of a late night infomercial. I want to bring out the real, dirty Emmy." Edgar smiled, knowing immediately he'd just coined a new nick-name.

"You just want an audience Edgar, don't lie."

"That's not true, Bev. Do you know me at all? I don't need to solicit an audience, they find me." Edgar wobbled as he spoke, and paused intermittently to chug directly from his tequila bottle. "I just…"

"Desperately need the affirmation?" Bev finished for him.

Edgar's eyes darted about as if the proper comeback might be found somewhere in the stillness of the night. "No. I just want people to have fun, babe. I want us all," he swung his arm in a broad circle as he spoke, "to have some memories to share later. You know, when we're old and rich and dead-fucking-sexy?" He poked Bev playfully in the side as he said this, and she laughed despite herself.

"Do you really think this was the best approach?" Bev pushed, even as her eyes softened and her posture relaxed.

"Hey, there you guys are!" The voice came from behind them. Turning, Edgar saw Alex trudging up into the light of the fire. He wore full winter garb: ski pants, coat, toque, boots—only the gloves were missing, his fingers over-occupied with the joint alternating between his hands and lips, and the large plastic kiddie-pool he balanced on his head.

Edgar, tolerating the weather in just a t-shirt and his leather jacket, immediately burst out laughing at the sight. "Alex, you idiot, where have you been?" he demanded, forgetting Bev immediately as he hurried towards his newly arrived friend.

"I found the yard you described alright," Alex explained, referring to Edgar's vague directions to a yard he'd noted earlier that week that contained the necessary pool, "It's just, I went to the wrong park afterwards is all," he finished, hanging his head.

Edgar grinned, letting his friend's mistake slide. Taking the pool from Alex, he heaved a loud sigh of relief. "Well," he said, gazing at the assembled materials and crowd, then over to Emeric, "are you ready to make some fucking memories?"

*****

All was silent in the great hall. Edgar's mouth trembled indecisively as he struggled to avoid letting loose the indignant laughter beating on the backs of his teeth.

He hadn't thought of that night for years, and if he hadn't just seen it, he'd have written it off as entirely forgotten.

It wasn't that bad, he assured himself, *besides, if anyone had ever needed to cut loose, it was Dirty Emmy.*

But it wasn't just the downtrodden humiliation on Emeric's face that echoed through his mind's eye now. It was Duncan's detachment, Bev's frustration. Even the poor, uncomfortable girls huddled together on the sidelines.

Gazing around, Edgar shuddered at the countless pillars awaiting him like the trees of some haunted forest.

He was moving before he ever chose a direction, passing pillar after pillar in a daze, trying his best to ignore the voices in his head. "Calm down, Edgar. Stop this, Edgar. You're going too far, Edgar. Edgar…"

"Edgar!"

For as long as he could remember, people had been warning him to slow down, to consider others, to take it easy: to take account of his actions. But everyone else did enough of that to cover him, and it had always fallen upon Edgar to ensure that his inner circle managed to glean at least a few decent experiences from their time together. *Someone had to provide some inspiration to the group. What else would we look back on?*

"Something to help you look forward, Mr. Vincent?"

"Pete, you fucker!" Edgar yelled. The man stood directly behind him, smiling graciously as he gestured to a table so laden with temptations, Caligula himself would've balked.

Bottles shimmered on its surface; crystal decanters filled with liquors of bronze, gold, and red. Tall piles of powder were stacked on silver trays, glass bongs with intricate swirling patterns awaited his indulgence, along with every other excuse Edgar could ever conceive of to do away with his mounting fatigue and welcome the dawn of a fresh new Saturday.

He shuddered. "No. Again no. And don't call me that," he doggedly replied.

Pete just smiled: a smug, self-certain smile that made Edgar twitch with rage. *Either that fucker just doesn't feel a thing, or…*

Edgar didn't bother to finish his thought. Wheeling about impatiently, he strode away, eager to put as much distance as possible between himself and the tantalizing offerings. They were only a crutch; a bit of entertainment better suited to happier times. This was a time for insight and reflection, a time for Edgar to find all the answers he so desperately needed.

It was something he had to do alone, and Edgar had little doubt he would accomplish the task if he could just stay focused. He'd always been able to find a way to get what he needed, and despite the cruel sense of unease gestating in his chest, Edgar was certain he knew what he needed just now. *Happier times,* he assured himself silently, *times when things made a bit more sense, when things worked like they were meant to.*

Pillars passed in silence as he walked. Then, like an unexpected alarm on an early Sunday morning, the world was spinning, and his arms whirled about at his sides in a frantic effort to regain his lost balance. The ground rolled underneath him, slipping away again and again until finally, just before he gave up the fight and accepted the fall, Edgar found his footing as dozens of tiny red and white beads rolled out from beneath him.

Following the trail of beads, he found himself standing beneath another towering colonnade. The concentration of beads beneath it confirmed it to be their source. They were accompanied by a pair of strings and two little brass crosses.

Rosaries, he knew instinctually. But he hadn't seen a rosary for ages. They were for penance, for confession. And it had been a long, long time since Edgar Vincent had confessed.

*****

"A boy who does not confess does not reconcile himself with the lord, mi rayo de sol. How can you ever expect to grow if you make choices like this?" His Nana's voice had been high and loud, her thick Argentinian accent rendering it all but indecipherable to anyone outside their immediate family.

"Tsk tsk, he's too young to understand such things, mi Madre. Leave him be or you'll only upset him." Edgar's mother always spoke quietly, but those who were wise took special care to listen to her soft words.

Edgar himself stood resolutely on the threshold of his bedroom. His tiny hands were slippery as they clenched into trembling fists, then released—ready at any provocation to slam the door shut and slide the chain-lock into place. Edgar was twelve, and as he listened intently to the back and forth between his mother and Nana, his youthful mind raced to calculate the best approach to accomplishing his goals.

Edgar had decided it the night prior—this was the day. Come hell or high water, this morning he would not be carted off with his mother and Nana to focus on how terrible he was, recite rhymes about his unworthiness, and expect to walk away feeling better.

His mother would come around. She always did, in the end. His Nana was a different story; old and hard, she would never understand how trying the long walk was, how much he hated the sight of that god-damned bell tower announcing that the time had come for blame and regret—and shitty music.

"Upset will be the least of his worries, mi hija. The boy must learn to

89

accept his faults and make account of himself. How else will he find his way in this world?"

Edgar placed one sweaty hand on his doorknob as the other fingered the guitar pick in his pocket. He glanced back at the shiny new guitar lying delicately on his bed. It had spent the night there, cozied up next to the boy as he tested each string again and again beneath his sheets.

It had been a gift from his father, and it changed his little world.

"By finding things out for myself!" he hollered, swallowing down the knot of fear in his throat. "Not by blaming myself for everything!"

His Nana had blessed herself thrice over, drawing his mother to her side with a comforting hand. Edgar meanwhile pulled the bright red pick out of his pocket, testing its strength between his fingers as he worried he may have overplayed his hand. His mother seemed upset now, but his Nana was furious, and one way or another, he knew at least that confession was no longer a threat.

A subtle smile passed over his angry young face. He hated arguments, and seeing his family upset was a hard thing to bear, but he just couldn't stand the idea of that long walk to tell a stranger about how bad he was; the tall, gothic steeple reaching up above the houses, calling out accusatory taunts with each step that brought him closer.

"A boy needs more than himself," Nana Vasquez insisted with a shake of her head. Edgar couldn't distinguish whether the crack in her tone was haughty or hurt. "Without faith Edito, a man is just a man. And what is that, after all?"

There were words between his Nana and mother at that point—all of them heated. But Edgar had no memory of them. He'd won, he knew, and stepping over the Sunday clothing that lay cast aside and wrinkled on the floor, he tumbled down onto his soft bed. Taking the shiny new instrument into his hands, he plucked one string, then another. He noted each sound, repeated the process once, and then moved on to the next string.

Lying alone, he'd moved his fingers up the fretboard, feeling the tight strings push into his soft flesh as he memorized the changes in tone.

"Are you OK?" The voice came from the door. Glancing up, Edgar found his mother awaiting him, a tray of cookies and glass of fresh lemonade in hand.

"Yes, Mom, I just wanted to be here today." He tore his attention away from the strings with a great effort and met his mother's gaze with unabashed sincerity. "With you."

Rosa's proud posture had collapsed in on itself like the end of a hard day and, setting down her tray, she'd lain on the bed and wrapped her arms around the little musician. "Oh Edgar, I know you must find your own way. It's OK, don't let Nana's words worry you. I'll always be here. Just don't lose your faith, my boy…everything will be alright."

Edgar didn't answer. He'd resumed plucking on the strings; his mouth splitting into a broad grin.

*****

Edgar had never gone to confession again. But he'd never lost his faith. Still, for the rest of his childhood, the threat of that tall church steeple loomed menacingly over all he did.

It wasn't about hurting anyone, just preserving myself. Edgar wondered why his insights were always accompanied by such strange remorse.

Few things in life had ever tried him quite as sorely as self-examination.

His Nana, admittedly, had always been a close competitor. Even in his earliest memories, she'd pushed him to change. His mother had as well, but that was always about being his best self—something at which Edgar always felt he excelled.

At least, he reflected, drifting listlessly between the pillars, *until this whole "death" fiasco.*

Edgar thought about his mother often, certainly far more often than he made the effort to visit. His phone calls on religious holidays—one of his few longstanding traditions—were his primary contact at this point.

Rosa had long since ceased her objections. She'd always been easy to placate.

Old memories, new regrets. Jake was right, Edgar reflected moodily, *for the afterlife, this cycle seems awfully familiar.*

"Pete," he called, finally concluding that Pete's little table of indulgences wasn't such a terrible idea after all. "Pete?" But Pete didn't appear.

Figures, Edgar ruminated, *that even my own imagination would let me down at this point.*

"Edgar." He heard his name like a whisper on the wind. But no wind ran through these timeless halls, so cavernous and vast. He stood alone in the infinite silence: no comfort, no respite, no salvation.

"Edgar."

The voice, or voices, were soft. Following their call, he passed between pillars like a dream with no hope of waking.

"Edgar."

Just ahead, a blurry mass was visible beneath one of the pillars, and as he struggled to focus upon it, he heard the call again, louder now and more insistent. "Edgar..."

The shapes at the pillar's base took form and clarity as he approached. Legs and arms, smiles and shining eyes. A tangled mess of skin and curves—a veritable harem of angels gazed longingly up at him from a spread of red satin pillows. In a unified motion, eerie in its perfect coordination, their lips moved to declare their shared desire: "Edgar."

Tyra was there, and Tiffany. Jasmine, Chanel, Leslie, and half a dozen others Edgar hadn't yet met. Each lay as if somehow comfortable upon the pillows and marble checkerboard of a floor, clothed in loose-fitting tunics like Edgar's own, their folds and stitches concealing little of the angels' promise.

Around their heads were wreaths, old and brown, with thorns jutting outward where they didn't push into the skin, tearing tiny bloodless holes into the angels' soft flesh.

They stared at him with hungry eyes, and their tongues were long and sharp as they flicked out over crimson lips. "Edgar," they called again.

Edgar smiled, his hands clenching nervously at his sides as he tried to ignore the chill in his blood.

The angels grinned back, their spines curving and their dark eyes flashing with satisfaction at his hollow gesture. *But that's all it ever took, was a smile. It was true of my mother, true of all the women I've met since...*

"Edgar," they called once more, and Tyra's knife-like nails played against the marble floor, indicating an empty spot for Edgar to curl into and join them.

He knew it was a terrible idea.

But Edgar had never been one to pass up an opportunity for satisfaction.

*****

The room had been lit by a sole lamp. Sitting at the edge of a misused bookshelf in Edgar's dorm room, the green banker's lamp had been a gift. He stared into it solemnly, letting its bright glow burn into his retinas as he rested his head in the warm lap of the gift-giver.

"Edgar," Bev spoke—finally putting to rest the stony silence that had extended since the basic greetings of her arrival. Edgar puffed on a cigarette. He wasn't meant to smoke in his dorm, but it was his second year now, and he figured exceptions could be made.

92

Bev coughed as a long waft of smoke floated up into her face, and took a drink of water from her canteen before continuing. "I don't even know what to say anymore."

Her eyes watered as she spoke, and her voice broke periodically, leading to long stretches of silence in which Edgar could smoke in peace.

"How are we supposed to keep going when nothing ever changes?" she finally asked.

Edgar groaned, taking another drag as he snuggled his head deeper into Bev's warmth. "That's just it, baby." His voice was deep and smooth, and he spoke with the dreamy, speculative distance otherwise reserved for showmen and shamans. "Nothing's changed. I'm still right here, and we're still having the same tired arguments." He took Bev's small hand in his own as he spoke, the green glow of the lamp casting a queer tint over the room.

"So why don't we just breeze over all the unpleasant arguing and get to the coupling in exquisite, carnal excess?" Edgar's tone rose endearingly, and he slid Bev's hand down his bare, trim stomach to the waistline of his jeans.

Bev pulled away, her head falling back against the unforgiving padding of Edgar's residence futon. "Dammit Edgar, wait! You have no patience for anything but satisfaction. I'm tired of it, it's really getting old. Power ballads and chocolates won't cut it this time. Something has to change. One thing or another."

"Oh, I have patience Beverly, don't you doubt that." The curl of his lip and twinkle in his eye assured Bev that he hadn't heard a word she'd said. "I know just when to wait," he whispered, allowing his hot breath to play along her neck and up towards her earlobe. Then, bringing his hand up from the floor, he held out a shot for his lady, "and just when to deliver," he finished with a dramatic flourish.

Bev sighed, turning her head away, rejecting the shot while trying to conceal her immense frustration.

Edgar took only one of the cues. Tossing the shot down his own throat, he shifted on the futon to better meet Bev's shimmering eyes. "That's why it'll be so great," he continued undeterred, "and why we really shouldn't wait any longer."

His hand passed gently up Bev's side as he rhapsodized. Before she could brush it away, however, there was a deafening pounding on the door.

"Yo Edgar, you home?" The booming, slurred voice came slamming into the room, shattering the awkward intimacy of the moment. "I found some bitches outside, you gotta come help me close the deal."

The voice was Jake's.

"Really Edgar? This guy again? Now?" Bev had not, in Edgar's opinion, had time to cultivate a fair and dynamic understanding of the plucky young high-school boy.

"That's Jake!" Edgar's eyes shone mischievously as he clarified for Bev. "He's got bitches," he continued, hoping against hope that Bev would appreciate his ironic humour.

Her defeated sigh told him she had not.

"You answer it," he instructed in an effort to distract from his insensitive comment.

But it just kept getting worse for poor Edgar, who saw instantly in Bev's expression that this plan had failed as well.

"I will not," she declared indignantly. "I barely know him. Besides, he's kind of creepy."

"C'mon babe," Edgar pressed, "just pretend I'm not here."

"Oh Edgar, sometimes I do," came her sad reply.

"What's that supposed to mean?" Edgar glanced up at Bev, but her eyes were elsewhere.

"Edgar?" Jake's voice was equal parts desperation and confusion.

"Jake," Edgar yelled doubtfully, as if into a portal to a beautiful world where choice and consequence were as yet unacquainted. "Just take them to The Scholar; buy them shots. You can do this, kid." Edgar considered for a moment before adding, "Try not to talk much."

Edgar waited, listening to the footsteps making their unsteady way down the hall.

"So," he said after he was certain they were gone, smirking as he gazed up at Bev's soft features, "are you ready?"

"Ugh," Bev moaned, shaking her head, "you're more concerned with getting your idiot friend laid than you are with us."

"That's not true, he just really needs the help. Besides, I brought him into the group, I can at least help him fit in. I helped Emmy, didn't I?"

"You publically shaved him." Bev reddened, and a tremble crept down her spine.

"Oh Bev, don't be all mad. He needed to learn to unwind. Besides, you know no one comes before you." He rolled over as he spoke, cuddling into Bev's chest as he flashed a salacious smile. "And if you don't know that…"

This time Bev did look down, staring angrily at Edgar, who relaxed immediately and happily latched onto her intense gaze. He watched as her rage shifted slowly into annoyance, then vulnerability. He knew he had it— Bev never could resist the confident sparkle of his eyes or his ingratiating smile.

"You're always so sure," she said, but the moody edge was gone from her voice now, and the angry slant of her eyebrows faltered as she strained in its upkeep.

"It's not just that, baby," he spoke quietly, making Bev lean in to hear him. "It's just that I'm ahead of other people, and I know what's going to happen…" He helped her close the distance as he spoke.

"Bro!" Along with the renewed pounding at the door, Jake's bellow caused Edgar to jump; head-butting Bev and sending them both rolling in pain and shock until they were tangled with one another in the cozy confines of the futon. "I've got no cash!"

The dumbfounded couple chuckled at this. "Get them to buy, that's bonus points," Edgar hollered in reply.

"Really?" The audible note of surprised excitement in Jake's voice renewed their laughter.

"Yes," Edgar answered, wrapping his arms around Bev, who gave a half-hearted show of resistance. "Now fuck off, I'm busy!"

"Such a supportive sensei," Bev teased.

"Baby birds got to fly eventually," he answered. After a moment's consideration, he added, "nice alliteration!"

Bev smiled, her hair tumbling down to entomb his face as she pushed herself up and stretched her tiny body out on top of his. "Edgar, who are you?"

"The one and only."

"Sometimes I wonder."

"What?" he asked, reaching up to tickle her cheek with the stubble of his close-cropped head.

"How you can be so many things? So smart, so passionate, so bold, and yet still such a farce? Every time I convince myself you're what I need, you go and prove me wrong. More booze, more absent nights, more strange women. Why can't you just pick what you want to be and stick with it?"

"You know I try, baby. I want to be everything you need, and more." He looked up at her as he spoke, feeling her breath against his chest as he ran his hands gently along her arms.

"But others always need me to be something else," he continued. "Like that idiot out there. I want to make everyone happy, and you more than anyone. But it's such a hard balance."

Bev's breath was coming faster now, her pupils dilating as Edgar took her supporting wrists into his hands affectionately. "But I'll get it right Bev, for you. You just have to have faith."

Bev opened her mouth to answer, but never got the chance. In that instant, Edgar pushed her wrists out from under her, bringing her tumbling down on top of him. With the same motion, he wrapped an arm around her, using it in conjunction with her momentum to roll over and envelope her in his embrace.

Her lips moved once more to protest, but were silenced by his own.

*****

The stinging burn on Edgar's tongue wasn't what he was expecting. It was much more familiar. Opening his eyes, he realized he couldn't even recall the taste of Bev's lips. There was an empty glass in his hand, and he tossed it away as he swallowed the mouthful of Jack, gratefully.

Pete's hoarse laughter was the real surprise, and as Edgar shook off the comfortable cobwebs of reminiscence, he watched the man's body lurch and sway with each loud guffaw.

The angels were gone, and Edgar stood beneath the twisting pillar alone with Pete, who held a diminishing bottle of Jack in one hand as the other extended a follow-up shot to Edgar.

He received it eagerly.

Some things never change.

Edgar's tunic was disheveled and torn, and as he adjusted it, he noticed a series of deep scratches along his chest. Pulling the fabric back into place, he felt evidence the damage was only worse on his back.

All the remorse with no memory of the pleasure—this place really has it ass-backwards. He took a drag from the cigarette in his hand. *This doesn't even merit a call to Emmy.*

Pete didn't speak. He barely even moved as his arm drifted out like one of the pillar branches: inevitable and immutable. He held another shot, which Edgar again took and consumed. Its warmth flowed through him, yet failed to chase out the growing chill.

"Thanks," said Edgar.

"Of course, sir," Pete answered, and now Edgar was certain of the malevolence lurking behind his cordial grin.

That smug bastard is definitely enjoying this. Can't a man just get some peace in...

Edgar bit his lip as he thought, not feeling the pain.

Memory and regret; choice and consequence; Saturday and Sunday. This whole Hall of Memories scene was a little too familiar for comfort. It was the same cyclical nightmare that had encompassed his days for far too long, bleeding together the blurry nights and blindingly bright mornings. Edgar wanted to leave, to escape from the pillared expanse and retreat to somewhere else, anywhere else.

He pinched his eyes shut and thought intently about The Scholar, but it did no good. When his eyes opened, the twisted pillars still sprawled off in all directions; and Pete held out another shot.

Edgar took it. He was tired of fond old memories tinged with new misgivings. Tired of Pete's mocking company. Sick-and-fucking-tired of being stuck in a limbo defined by his own excess.

But I've been trying to change things. Edgar was certain of that.

"What do you intend to do now, Mr. Vincent?" asked Pete, pouring another shimmering bronze stream of booze into a tiny crystal shot glass.

Edgar stared into the glass as he took it from Pete. *What do I intend to do?* he wondered.

His reflection bent around the glass in a surreal way. Distorted by the savoury liquid within, his features morphed into a mask barely recognizable as himself.

Behind the reflection, another pillar waved and throbbed through the murky brown tint of the Jack. Superimposed behind his own mutated face, it hovered as if just beyond reach, vying for his attention with barbed claws.

Edgar focused on his image. *Handsome bastard,* he mused.

He smiled, but the relief he hoped for did not come. No matter the depths of depravity to which he had sunk in the past, he'd always been able to allow his childish sincerity to flow forth in the most disarming way. It had helped him satisfy many justifiably angry people throughout his life, yet his own happiness had always been a different matter.

What does it take to really satisfy yourself? he wondered, knowing the answer had always been easier than he'd let on.

But I've been working on that too, he thought. He'd been trying to make the most of his potential; it had been priority number one, in fact.

If only I hadn't died when I did, he reflected somberly. But that wasn't it either. There was never enough time, no matter how much time he had.

But I was trying, he reassured himself as if repetition would settle his doubts. *I was trying…*

*****

The bar had been an abysmal sort of place. All abstract art and brightly-lit floors. Bathrooms with tip-expectant attendants and quiet jazz music. Women with long dresses and bad attitudes. It was the type of bar Edgar wouldn't have been caught dead in during university except on some mad dare. But Edgar had been out of university for seven years now, and as a man of 29, his options were dwindling steadily.

Emeric had actually bargained for The Scholar, being that he lived and worked on campus, and seldom ventured beyond it for any reason aside from all-inclusive family vacations.

Insular little man, Edgar had thought. He hadn't voiced the opinion however, as he too had been pressing for The Scholar—being that he was eager to meet the new batch of students who would just be arriving.

So much for that, he'd reflected.

Sadly, Duncan had won out in the end. So, the three of them sat at an obnoxious white prism of a table, balancing precariously on uncomfortably tall stools at a club called Débit de Boissons.

The backs of the stools were insufficient to support an actual back. Edgar's battered old coat hung limply from its subtle curvature, its sleeves brushing against the polished floors. He fussed with it anxiously, now pulling it forward, now sliding it back to find the right placement. "My feet can't reach the floor, yet my jacket can't avoid it! Why on Earth would you ever come here?"

"I was hoping to teach you some class, but I've no doubt I was over-bold," said Duncan, grinning. "So," he continued between fragile sips of his olive-reeking martini, "how is this new project of yours coming along? You seemed pretty enthusiastic about it when last we spoke."

"You know," Edgar started with a flourish of excitement. Then, noticing the off-putting enthusiasm with which Emeric watched him, dialed it back and continued, "it's pretty good."

"C'mon Edgar, don't hold out on us. There must be something special about this one?" Emeric asked, crushing the lime down into his drink with a striped straw.

"Jesus man, you talk like it's a lady." Edgar glanced over at Duncan, but received no response.

Jake was out of town that night.

"Edgar, how I long for the day I can honestly ask you that about a woman," Emeric said with a smirk.

At that, Duncan did laugh. *Treacherous bastard,* Edgar thought with a pout concealed by an old fashioned—minus the orange.

"No really, it's coming very well," he reiterated, nervously fussing with his jacket in a futile attempt to prevent it from brushing against the floor.

"It's been what, almost a year now? Just over? Is there a due date in sight?" asked Duncan. "I know you like to age your scotch before the big day Edgar, but…"

Duncan knew him far too well. Edgar grinned, "This one's pretty open-ended. The director is utterly in my debt for taking the project on, so I've more or less got free reign from here on out. The film is already assembled and laid out on the slab. It's really going to be something, and it's up to my music to give it the jolt which brings it to life."

"But, if you're so far above this project, I'm left wondering why you're doing it in the first place. What drew you to this one?" Emeric asked.

"Yeah," said Duncan, twirling his tall martini glass between three fingers, "what is your selling point here? You talk about it like some Holy Grail of projects. What was it called again? BHI?"

"BHI, yeah. *Basic Human Indecency.* And it is special, although I can't quite put my finger on why."

"An indie film from an unknown director, the appeal of which you can't even elucidate? I'm not sure this sounds like the meal ticket you've been looking for, my friend," Duncan said with a chiding smile.

"It's more of a documentary, really," Edgar corrected feebly. "And I don't necessarily expect it to be a big money maker. That's not why I'm doing it."

Duncan arched his eyebrows, an incredulous expression on his face.

Emeric started to speak, but then stopped himself, scratching his forehead to conceal his doubtful expression. "So, what is it then?" he finally asked.

"Well, part of it is for my career, I admit." Edgar pushed a hand into his back pocket as he spoke, paused, and frowned. Looking over at Duncan, he offered his friend an apologetic grin. Duncan sighed as he withdrew a shiny silver cigarette case from his breast pocket, tapped it twice against the table and took out a smoke each for Edgar and himself. The one benefit of Duncan's ritzy private clubs was that the constraining rules of public domains did not apply.

Taking the smoke and lighting it with an appreciative nod, Edgar continued, "Look, I'm still taking on side projects to maintain my disposable income; easy shit that takes no real effort, you know. BHI is just a chance to do something a bit more meaningful. Lucrative or not, I know that when I get this project just right, it's going to show the industry what I'm capable of—my real potential.

"Beyond that, it's the project itself that gets me. There's a real honesty to it. It's the kind of film that really makes you examine yourself and society in general. I think there's a really good message to it, and I'm just happy for the opportunity to be involved. If I can make it better with my music, that alone would be worth my time. I just," he concluded, puffing thoughtfully on his smoke, "I just need to get it right."

Emeric stole a quick sip of his rum and coke, then glanced dubiously up at his old friend. "Well, if that's the case, then I'm happy for you Edgar. I truly hope this is the passion-project you've been waiting for."

Duncan, however, was never such an easy sell. "I'm glad you're getting so much out of this Eds, it sounds like a very personal job for you. But I hope you've thought about your long-term direction. We all know how talented you are—your resume alone is proof of that. But lately you have to admit you've been taking projects which are beneath you, and this one's been in limbo for quite a while now."

Edgar sighed. "Look," he said, "I've heard it claimed that you have a lifetime to create your first great project and your last. You get noticed—then you start to consider your legacy. Everything else is on a schedule. But you guys know I'm a trendsetter! I'm just trying to buck the norm and take my time with this. It may not be my last project, but it damn sure could be my greatest, and that alone makes it worth as much time as it takes."

Duncan rolled his eyes—he'd never had much patience for what he considered "empty talk and shallow platitudes."

"That all sounds great, mon frère. Still, you've got to keep your profile up, or you're never going to achieve the goals you used to have."

"'Used to have'?" Anger flashed in Edgar's eyes. "Why 'used to?' You start taking showers in money, and you think that's all there is. But this is about more than that for me. It's about how I want to live. The man I want to be."

Duncan's thin lips pursed together briefly, and he took a long sip from his martini. When he finally spoke, his voice was cool and even. "And when does that begin exactly? You'll happily tell anyone who'll listen about how damn special you are, and how much you have to offer deep down. But it's not as if the assent of one more stranger will ever amount to sufficient proof for you to finally start acting like it."

Emeric stared silently into his drink, reaching up periodically to adjust his glasses.

"It has begun, my friend. That's what I'm doing here. I know you can't understand that. I mean, sure, you'll live in a mansion when you're older, but you'll still sit in it and fantasize about all the great things you'd do if you still had your youth!"

"And what about you?" Now Duncan's eyes flashed, but still his voice remained calm. "Where will you be when you're older? Sitting in some bar, hoping the women will still answer to the wink of your tired old eye? Finding new friends in an alley somewhere?"

Edgar huffed. "That sounds so terrible to you, doesn't it? The truth is I've met more decent people in bars and backstreets than I have in law firms or on campuses." Emeric's shoulders slouched at this mention. "And I've had plenty from all, believe me."

Duncan took another drink before he answered: "Ignoring the disturbing distinction between 'met' and 'had,' I find myself wondering if perhaps you're confusing 'decent' with these hypothetical people's ability to tolerate your bullshit?"

Edgar sneered, then chuckled through grinding teeth. Emeric, meanwhile, looked up from his cup of melting ice cubes. "Edgar, you've walked all those avenues and more…are you still one of the decent people?"

The dark ridges of Duncan's eyebrows rose in surprise, and he pointed matter-of-factly at Emeric. "That's actually a much better question."

Edgar said nothing. He simply sat and stared, savouring the last few drags of his borrowed cigarette.

"Edgar," it was Duncan who broke the silence, "I'm not trying to shit on your ambitions here, you know that. It's just that I care about you, buddy. If this project is really all you say it is, then I'm thrilled you're dedicating yourself to it. I just don't want to see you so lost on an idea that you forget about reality. I want you to be and have everything you dream of Edgar, that's all."

Edgar nodded his head. "This one's really going to mean something, Duncan, old pal. This one… Well, you'll see." He frowned pensively and finished his old fashioned with a long, deep swallow.

*****

Edgar swayed in place, his sense of balance as uncertain as the ever-shifting pillars. The shot glass in his hand was empty now, and he let it drop to the marble floor.

A cigarette hung limply from his lips, and a trail of grey smoke rose from it, floating easily away in the warm, still air. Edgar always had something to say, and considered it his profound duty to do so in every situation, appropriate or not.

But just now, Edgar was speechless.

The disordered rows of pillars rolled off into the distance, and he walked through them unburdened by intention, needing only to move.

They stretched up all about him, blacks and greys and whites, their monolithic size making him feel utterly insignificant in a realm that depended on him entirely.

His steps began to quicken, and he perceived the pillars pressing in, as if at any moment they would slam together, entrapping him in an eternal tomb of his own vague recollections.

His tunic rubbed uncomfortably at his thighs as he began to run, turning this way and that to avoid long enclosures of pillars. It would be too easy to turn down any one of them, to face the truths inside and never again come out.

Staggering as he ran, Edgar navigated through the empty spaces of his mind. He sped through long, gloomy stretches, always under the terrible shadows of the columns. Striving against his will, he vied to keep his eyes ahead and unfocused as they fought of their own accord, drifting from side to side to settle upon the lurid artifacts at the pillar bases.

There were dirty, empty bottles, and broken instruments. He saw an old chandelier, a long chain of handcuffs, and more than one display that made even Edgar blush. At the periphery of his vision, he made out what appeared to be a long thin sheet of yellow plastic wrapped around one pillar's base. *The fucking Slip-n-Slide*, he realized, cursing his friends' chiding laughter as it echoed through his mind.

He didn't slow down. With each turn he took, the pillars drew closer, constricting his course, culling his choices. Stumbling, Edgar caught sight of the checkerboard pattern below him and felt suddenly that he was the lone king, sorely beset by enemies of his own creation.

Alone and hunted, Edgar was overwhelmed by a strange sense of familiarity. *I've done this all before,* he knew.

Cutting around a shaft that rose up suddenly in his path, he staggered between two others pushing in from opposite directions. Barely squeezing through, he noticed in passing a lone photo hanging upon one. The eyes were burned out by cigarette tips, but despite the defacement and dust, Edgar knew the image was Duncan.

He remembered the photo well—his friend standing tall and proud in his black robe, clutching his diploma like a sword as he set forth on his noble crusade.

"You've got to stay focused Edgar, I'm not about to cow my bragging on your account. So get busy and catch up so we can rule this world together, old buddy. Don't let it get away from you." The day that Duncan had passed the bar, Edgar had emptied one—of wares and women alike.

Now he dodged through his own sordid past, his mind racing to understand how such a surreal scene could be so terribly familiar. A glimmer to the right caught his eye. At the base of a pillar sat a delicate silver necklace, its broken heart pendant coolly reflecting the dichotomous pattern of the marble floor.

Edgar remembered giving the charm to Bev. He remembered when she finally gave it back. "Edgar, I'm not coming out tonight. Not anymore. You're never going to change, and I can't watch you continue to ruin yourself. The real shame is that you're wasting such potential…you could have been so special, if only you didn't keep getting lost in your own story."

He'd let the necklace drop from his hand and walked away. He'd never seen Bev again.

I thought it was a waste of time to pursue someone who didn't believe in me, he recalled.

Biting his lip, he noticed in the distance one pillar rising up above all the rest. It was much thicker and far taller, and its twisting branches jutted out sharply, weaving like razors up and up over Edgar's deranged reality. The pillar reached and beckoned, horrifying in its enormity, becoming the centre point of Edgar's world as he turned his steps towards it.

A pillar to his left was arrayed with red Christmas lights, numbered Ping-Pong balls taped to them at intervals. A heave of his stomach forced a slight smirk to his lips as he recalled his personally-designed drinking game, Fuck Emmy.

But beneath the pillar to his right sat a broken set of glasses. He remembered the disappointment on Emeric's face as he'd scooped them up from the mud and filth of a rundown alley one cold Sunday morning.

"Edgar, every time I listen to your pleas for trust, I end up getting hurt somehow. You need to learn that your choices affect other people."

He shook the voice from his head, the great spire drawing incrementally closer as he hurried toward his inevitable doom.

"It's really not such a long walk when you know who waits for you, mi rayo de sol," his Nana's pitched voice was in his ear now.

His spine was ice, but the air was thick and hot. Gazing at the great pillar as he plowed onward, Edgar couldn't shake his growing feeling of unease, and as the monolith shook and shimmered, he feared he was not ready to receive whatever revelation might await him.

But the other pillars were pressing closer, and his options were running out. They rose up all around him, each ornamented with all manner of trinkets, mementos, and photographs.

"You will make me proud when I'm gone, Edgar. I know it," his father's voice droned softly from a rum stained photo ahead of him.

"Fuck yeah, Edgar, this is the kind of shit that proves you'll be remembered forever!" Jake's loud, monotone voice boomed in his head as he caught sight of a long rope fashioned from women's underwear hanging down from the end of a huge balloon bearing his university's logo.

Remembered forever...

The columns had him boxed in completely now. The great spire was just ahead, yet entirely beyond his reach.

"Edgar, I'm worried about you. You've got to get control..." Duncan's voice again. *Always fucking Duncan.*

"I know you will get there Edito," he heard his mother say from a pillar accompanied by an old rotary phone on a fine wooden end-table. "I just pray you know where you're going."

Where am I going? Edgar wondered, wrestling again with the eerie familiarity of his run towards the spire. *I was trying to get somewhere,* he realized.

"Don't worry, Ma," he'd answered into his cellphone as he waved over a dancer wearing only a Santa hat. "I'm working on it; things are going to turn around soon."

Turn around! That was it. The night of his death was flashing before him like strobe lights and stop-motion. He'd tried to stop it. He'd tried to turn around, but it had been too late.

It took a moment to summon the courage. The weight of everything he'd seen pressed down on his shoulders, and doubt glued the soles of his shoes, making turning a nearly insurmountable act of will. Finally, he managed, and as he watched the great spire rotate out of view, Edgar found a new pillar before him. Pete stood beside it. His silver hair was disheveled and pointed; his Cheshire smile wrapping around his thin face like the comforting embrace Edgar so desperately longed for.

"Why am I here, Pete?"

Pete laughed—long and loud and full of hateful judgment. "Where is it you think you are, Mr. Vincent?"

Edgar knew both questions were his own and swallowed down the common answer knotted in his throat.

Then the display at the pillar's base was all that remained of his world. Small candles, many unlit, ran along the edge of a delicate table laden with a pristine white cloth. Wreaths and flowers sat within the circle of candles, and at the epicenter was a photo of Edgar, the flickering flames of the burning candles reflecting in his eyes.

He was smiling in the picture, which sent a pang of anguish through his chest.

This is what's left of me down there, he understood, and his gaze lingered on the unlit candles.

*I always had the best intentions...*Edgar tried to convince himself.

He failed.

This is all wrong; I've made mistakes, sure. But I'm better than this. With a huff, he determined to take back control. The afterlife was the result of his own expectations after all, and now he needed to turn those towards what really mattered.

He fought to remind himself of the candles that were lit and the people who had never let go.

Edgar knew what he needed to do. He needed to get his friends together and remember the good times rather than the bad. He needed to focus on the future and all the fine things he'd meant to accomplish in it. More than anything, he needed to remember what was really important in the life he'd lost.

I need a fucking party...

CHAPTER 8
THE GALA IN HONOUR OF THE LIFE AND TIMES OF EDGAR VINCENT

Social gatherings for Edgar Vincent had always been an opportunity to allow some of his greatest talents to shine forth. Obviously, bars were a prime example of this phenomenon. Since his first time at a bar—an adventure supported by Duncan and facilitated by a shoddy pair of fake IDs—Edgar had viewed them as the ideal forum for his charm and charisma.

This trait wasn't limited to bars of course.

Lecture halls in university had often become audiences for Edgar to spin captivating stories and woo naïve women.

House parties, more often than not, became congregations ripe for him to try out new routines and seize the attention of those in attendance, turning them to his own purposes.

At a charity function for Duncan's legal firm, Edgar had once focused his efforts on conducting a little social experiment. Introducing himself by a different name—each accompanied with a unique and sordid backstory— to a choice selection of women in attendance, he then kept track of how many times someone else made reference to one of the false identities, and ultimately declared a "winner."

The winner in this case, being the woman proven to have spoken the most about Edgar in his absence, was invited to accompany him as he made a hasty retreat from the mounting confusion.

She'd accepted, although she never did manage to discover his true identity.

Edgar's endeavours weren't always so self-serving, however. When he had finished the score for his first feature film, he'd used his speech—in addition to a video he'd assembled for the occasion—to drop countless barely subliminal messages about the legendary sexual prowess of his invited guest, Emeric.

It hadn't worked out quite as he later claimed he'd intended, but the raucous laughter enjoyed by everyone aside from Emeric had at least made for a memorable night.

Unfortunately, the results weren't always so agreeable. Over the years, work-related functions had become harbingers of disaster for Edgar. However, they were also amazing opportunities to advance his career, rub elbows with producers, and, ideally, rub up against some young starlets as well. These potential benefits made such events hard to resist, but Edgar's latent talent for making a scene came with some significant drawbacks as well. When, at just such a soiree, he'd been caught in the bathroom with the girlfriend of the head writer, Edgar had quickly surmised that his ambitious decision to attend was undermined by his inability to control his desires.

That project hadn't worked out.

No matter, Edgar had thought, *it wasn't the right job anyway.*

Edgar was a difficult man to keep down and so at the next work function, he'd decided to circumvent the risk and even the playing field by spiking the punch. Upon finding, much to his chagrin, that the Hollywood portrayal of a central punch bowl was less than accurate, Edgar had simply endeavoured to spike every available drink, soup, and condiment he could find. Inevitably, the entire affair fell apart under the drunken and despicable shenanigans that resulted.

Again, Edgar lost his job, but he remained certain everyone on the set would remember his name for the rest of their undoubtedly dull lives.

There was no question about it; be it a bar, a wedding, a convocation, or a simple night out, Edgar knew how to command attention.

"—fucker!" The boom of Edgar's scream echoed through the Golden Ballroom, the fairy-dance tinkling of the shot glass he hammered into the floor its only accompaniment. Then, both faded into a stony silence.

But the night hadn't started out so bleak for Edgar. As a matter of fact, he'd started his evening, as he did so very many others, with the best of intentions.

*****

"I'm here!" Edgar announced as he strode merrily through the foggy threshold into the warm embrace of the Golden Ballroom. He wondered as he walked if the depth of meaning he'd intended would be understood by the bustling crowd of friends and angels awaiting him.

Unlikely, he decided, *but I've got time to clarify. That is why I'm here, after all.*

If the ballroom was lavish the last time he'd visited, Edgar noticed immediately that the flare had been turned up an admittedly feeble notch.

The tall, vaulted walls of gold were adorned here and there with a rainbow of streamers, and floral arrangements littered the sparse tables. At equally spaced intervals along the dark wooden bar sat bowls—also gold—filled with shiny decorative balls of every colour, and in the upper corner of each wall there was a collection of bright balloons, somewhat deflated and limp. They hung listlessly, like flowers near to death.

Discordant music played softly; a menagerie of violins and horns all sputtering and yelping tunelessly as a fireplace full of cats.

Everyone in attendance was elegantly dressed as Edgar navigated through the tightly packed angels on his way to the bar in search of his friends. Unfortunately, the dress code extended to himself. To Edgar's extreme annoyance, his trusted leather coat was conspicuously absent, a fine black suit jacket filling its stead. Below it was an unadorned white collared shirt and a pair of dark, freshly pressed slacks.

No tie, Edgar noted with relief, *at least there's no fucking tie.*

Straightening the collar of his outfit with a quick jerk, he stretched out and smiled. He'd set out with the sole intent of making account of his past mistakes, hoping this gesture would render the remainder of his afterlife a little more pleasant. *A bit less flare and more class would have helped.* There was no trace of irony in his silent observation. *But it'll do.*

Since his trials in the Hall of Memories, Edgar felt charged with a reinvigorated sense of purpose. He'd learned a lot about himself from the experience and now felt like a new man: ready to make amends; work towards self-improvement; and, above all, to finally be the man he'd always told people he was beneath the distractions.

Tacky digs be damned, nothing will prevent me from setting things right, vowed Edgar. Running his fingers nervously along the neatly tailored sleeves of his suit jacket, he elbowed his way through the crowd.

"Nice setup, Eds." The sudden sound of Duncan's sarcastic voice sent a shudder of panic through Edgar's tired body, and he stood for a moment perplexed, worrying that his friend's disembodied voice had returned to plague him with homilies and platitudes even in his moment of triumph.

But that wasn't the case, and a sigh of relief broke from Edgar's dry lips when he located the source of the voice through the crowded environs of the Golden Ballroom.

It had been years since Edgar was so happy to see the sardonic smile of his suave compatriot. That Duncan stood in the welcome company of the rest of his inner circle—and next to a long line of shots laid out on the bar—was just the icing on the cake for the party Edgar had deigned to dream up this fine Saturday night.

"Nice tie, Duncan," Edgar's glib response fell flat under his obvious tone of contentment.

"Good to see you," he added earnestly. Tonight was all about appreciating the good things in life and, although Duncan was often a source of great frustration to Edgar, he knew he couldn't come to terms with his past without having his oldest friend at hand.

Emeric smiled, holding up his highball glass by way of welcome. Jake thrust his own beer out in an approximation of the gesture, sending a quick splash down to the floor as he forced a foamy belch.

"Hey Edgar, good to see you man." Alex spoke through purple lips as he held out his half-empty wine glass.

Duncan passed a fresh glass of brandy to Edgar, then took a sip from his own glass—scotch, Edgar reasoned. Duncan and Edgar shared a supreme distaste for partaking of the same drink as anyone in their company. "Ready and waiting for you, mon frère," said Duncan, but whether he was referring to the drinks or the company, Edgar couldn't be certain. "Heaven's got to have some perks, after all."

Edgar accepted the drink gratefully, a pensive expression spreading like a cloud over the sunlight of his newfound optimism. "I'm not so sure this is heaven brother, but let's not let that bog us down."

Raising his cup to meet the rest, Edgar noticed Jake leering eagerly at Emeric, an excited grin spreading across his broad face.

Jake never smiles at Emmy, he noted with a start. He realized his error a second later.

"But first thing's first, boys." Edgar didn't really expect he'd be sitting anytime soon, but with a gesture to the long line of shots waiting on the bar behind them, determined not to hang himself on the finer points of tradition.

Emeric smiled with the unrestrained joy of a schoolboy who's just discovered a peephole between the locker rooms, "I told you he wouldn't forget. I win!" He spoke sidelong to Jake as he busily distributed shots from the near-limitless supply on the bar.

"I don't feel like I lost," Jake answered, staring hungrily at his fistfuls of booze. Alex giggled at this as he accepted his own shot.

"Well Edgar," said Duncan, and the circle of men held their shots up in anticipation, "to what do we drink tonight?"

Taking in the warm faces surrounding him, a faint flush crept into Edgar's cheeks. *You know,* he thought, *this isn't too bad at all.*

With friends aplenty and drinks for days, he could hardly help second-guessing his earlier declaration to Duncan. *If this isn't heaven...*

"This one...," Edgar declared, raising his shot in answer as he looked upon each friend in turn. Alex: the glassy-eyed man had always understood Edgar's artistic goals and rebellious streak better than anyone. Jake: the most pig-headedly loyal man Edgar had ever met. Emeric: easily the kindest person Edgar knew, he never failed to expect greater decency from Edgar than he usually received.

Finally, there was Duncan; his most honest and caring critic. Duncan's thriving law career kept him terribly busy these days, and as such, the rare times he and Edgar did get to hang out together had lost much of the old magic. *It's as if he's compelled to condense all his ridiculous lectures and guilt-trips down into those infrequent doses*, Edgar mused.

Still, he knew Duncan meant well, and that beneath the chastising, he'd never really stopped believing that Edgar would someday join him to rule the world together.

"This one is to all of you," Edgar finished affectionately.

The glasses were clinked, then tapped, and the shots neatly put back with a unified series of contented "ahh's."

The shot was sweet and smooth as it coursed down Edgar's throat.

"I've been through a lot since coming here. I feel like I've lived three lifetimes," Edgar declared as he set his empty shot glass down on the bar and switched his brandy back to his right hand. "It's really been eye-opening, as I suppose any afterlife worth its salt should be."

He took a long swallow of brandy, working to corner the frantic thoughts scurrying about his mind. Standing in silence, he turned his head, visually scouring the hall. Angels danced and drank, and the lusty eyes of all were constantly transfixed on him alone, as if awaiting only a nod to come flocking to his side.

Golden beads dangled down from the high ceilings, and rows of golden chalices were arranged above the bar. Golden specks littered the dark floor, but it wasn't gold Edgar was searching for.

Not a trace of silver, he observed, not really knowing why.

"I was in a strange place earlier. It was terrible and amazing. There were giant pillars and countless altars dedicated to my past. I looked back all through my life and saw long-forgotten moments just like I was there. It really hit me hard, guys.

"I realize I haven't always been the friend you've all deserved, and I intend to correct that." The inner circle listened intently as he spoke. "I'm here today with a newfound sense of peace. In truth, I really think I'm reaching a point where I can accept the past and be at rest. Once I resolve a few more issues, I'll finally be able to be the "me" I've always intended—the true, ideal Edgar!"

A sudden howl brought his attention sharply over to the right, where the familiar marble statue appeared to have been cleared out in favour of a gigantic, steaming abomination.

Its core was like a gargantuan golden keg, supported and manipulated by three long, screeching pistons. Its head—for lack of a better term—was a dead television set, with beams of yellow light playing off the smooth contours all around the red coals of its eyes.

A Golden Bull? That would be just as well suited to a china shop, Edgar thought with a derisive chuckle. He was a man who appreciated juxtaposition as well as any—and better than most—still, it struck him as an especially discouraging sign. "Bars with Bulls," after all, had become a catchphrase between Jake and himself, used to draw particular attention to the sort of women the pair might hope to find in them and the related talents that could be deduced therein.

Come on Edgar, no distractions, he silently encouraged himself. *Just stay focused. You have a lot to accomplish here tonight and can't afford to get distracted by such trivial vices.*

"Wheeeeee!" The squeal came again from the tiny figure wrapped around the contraption's bulk like the desperate grip of a terrified child. Tiffany's eyes rolled like a roulette wheel, and she yelped and wretched as the machine whipped her about like a ragdoll. Its frame emitted noxious jets of steam from wheezing joints as she clung to its long, sharp horns like her life depended on it.

The inner circle watched this sight in quiet, dumbfounded awe. Edgar gritted his teeth in silent rumination, a perturbed expression scarring his handsome visage. "As I was saying," he continued proudly, once he was certain he'd regained the attention of his friends, "you're about to witness the second coming of Edgar Vincent."

"Been there." The lurid voice in his ear belonged to Tyra, who ran her reptilian tongue suggestively over shining lips as her carmine form slid past him towards the bar.

Damn angels, Edgar thought moodily.

"Those are some uncharacteristically noble ambitions, Eds. It sounds like you've really grown," said Duncan.

Edgar bit his lip, allowing the memories to ferment. "Yeah Duncan, looking back over all my choices like that—it's a lot to take in. Especially now, knowing that it's all said and done, and nothing can be changed.

"I learned about my death too," he continued absently, "not all of it mind you, but I know now that I was alone when I died, and that I tried to turn around somehow...just before the end."

A crash behind them robbed the triumph from Edgar's gestating redemption tale. Turning with a frustrated huff, he saw a little white mess covered in yellow polka-dots sprawled beneath the now-vacant mechanical monstrosity. The gaggle of angels packed around began to slowly disperse. Several lingered, rambunctiously attending to Tiffany's bent and motionless body.

The golden bull settled back onto its stand with a great hiss, towering above the room as the last spurts of steam snaked out from its joints and dissipated up towards the vaulted ceiling.

Edgar rolled his eyes, and continued only after a long draw from his brandy cup. "That's what tonight is about. It's hard to believe a guy like me could have died alone, I know. But it's true. And hell, maybe I deserved it. But I want to make a change—I need to. It's time I make up for some of my past mistakes.

"I know I haven't always been honest with all of you." Edgar gazed over at Alex as he spoke, the dishonesty of their first encounters casting a deep shadow over his mood. "I always felt like a leader of sorts, as if it was my duty to create memories and provide inspiration to you sorry saps. I wanted to give you stories to tell your children later on or to reflect on when life inevitably grew familiar and tedious. But I know that in the process I've also kept myself from you. I've always maintained this enigmatic ideal of who I am and held you all at arm's length to protect that.

"It wasn't my intention—such things are never planned. But I am sorry, nonetheless." Edgar beamed as he finished and straightened his back, a great weight lifting from his shoulders.

"Hey, that's OK, man," said Alex soothingly. "We understood it was just sort of scary for you to be honest sometimes. We don't hold it against you, guy."

"While that is true, Edgar, and we have only ever wanted you to be your best self," said Duncan, a wicked grin percolating beneath his cool demeanour, "tradition does dictate that we cannot formally forgive you without proper penance."

Edgar's smile vanished like a pleasant fragrance met by a sudden gale. *Duncan, you bastard,* he cursed his snake of a friend, but knew he had no argument to make. "Shots of Contrition" were a strict ritual established long ago at Edgar's own insistence, when Emeric had once made the mistake of admitting his choice of bar may have been less than ideal.

These fucks have never missed an opportunity to turn it on me ever since, Edgar fumed as he accepted a shooter of dark spirits from Duncan.

To a man, his friends watched with childish joy as he raised the glass and cleared his throat. Then, with a long sigh and exaggerated roll of his eyes, he fell seamlessly into the old routine. "For my thoughtless deceptions and misguided pretensions; my dishonesty, cowardice, and naive intentions, I do hereby supplicate myself." The shot was thick as he pounded it back, and its bitter flavour left his throat feeling hot and dry. He set the empty glass down on the bar and forced his mouth into his best approximation of a modest smile.

"That was real pretty, Edgar," Jake said between hoarse guffaws. The inner circle expressed their agreement with a tirade of cheerful laughter.

"It really is great to see such humility. I'm proud of you, Edgar," said Emeric.

"Oh f—" Edgar caught himself before reacting to Emeric. Shuddering as he recalled the callous and self-serving man he'd been shown in the Hall of Memories, he refocused with a quick swallow of brandy and continued with a smile.

"I know I've been a bit of a dick to you guys on occasion and you most of all, Emmy. I hope that's not how you remember me down there. When I look back on it now, I want to believe I was trying to make you stronger, to prepare you for the trials of life. It wasn't to be hurtful. Well, at least that wasn't the sole purpose. It wasn't right, I know, but it was always meant to have some kind of meaning."

Emeric pushed at his glasses, an uncertain expression on his freckled face. "Well, Edgar, it may have had meaning to you, but it did still get under the skin sometimes."

"It seems meaning and malignancy tread a fine line these days." Edgar frowned. "Nevertheless, I mean it—you're a great group of friends, and I'm deeply sorry I've been so shitty to all of you."

Edgar was on a roll and had rarely felt so proud of himself. His first threesome, his first completed score, and the one time he'd managed to not only bed a well-known model, but also make a stalker of her—were the only competing occasions that sprang to mind.

The feeling didn't last, however, and when Edgar caught the malicious smile on Emeric's weaselly face, a hot blade slashed up his back. His spine coiled and fists clenched, but the racing train of his desperation hit a brick wall as the smarmy little man giddily extended another dark shooter to him.

"Fuck you, Emmy! You deserved it all!" Jake erupted.

Emeric shrank back fearfully. Duncan and Alex watched in contented silence.

"No, no." Edgar accepted the shooter, ruefully breaking the tension with a delicate balance of facetiousness and contempt. "For my cruel jokes and selfish justifications; my ignorant self-focus and total lack of vindication, I do hereby supplicate myself." The shot was like fire, and a barking cough exploded from his lips as he finished it, placing the empty glass on the bar next to the others.

"Sorry Edgar, I just couldn't resist," Emeric said with a sheepish grin.

"Well done," said Duncan, giving the bespectacled man a firm clap on the back.

A long series of cheers and applause announced the exit of Tiffany, who limped out with her waifish arms wrapped around Jasmine and Leslie.

"With pigtails like that, you'd think she'd know how to ride," whispered Tyra with a wink. She pinched Edgar's posterior and carried a tray of drinks back towards the bull. Chanel was climbing up onto its broad back now, her white and orange stripes rippling, and the eager crowd of ethereally beautiful angels was pressing in close once again.

Every shape, shade and sexual proclivity was answered for in their ranks. Angels walked half-naked, licking their lips as their hands played over their exposed flesh. Others carried wide platters loaded with drinks and wore sensual expressions that left no doubts as to the depths of their service.

All were eerily inhuman, with long pointed nails and tongues that flicked like serpents. Their curves were exaggerated beyond realistic proportions, and their physical features shifted as Edgar watched them, morphing in a constant search for satisfaction. One angel blended into the next like streetlights on a drunken walk home; an endless smorgasbord of surreal temptations.

But amid the harrowing visions, Edgar strove for a sight of silver. *Bev,* her name echoed in his head now. He didn't know what he'd say to her if she were to appear, only that in times of turmoil, the mind often returned to old comforts.

I was never such a comfort to her though, he knew, remembering again the thoughtless actions he'd witnessed in the Hall of Memories.

"So, Edgar, what did you see, anyway?" asked Alex from behind absent eyes, "What's made you start re-evaluating everything like this?"

Edgar ruminated on his experiences—his first meeting with Alex; his heretical defiance as a child; old plans and familiar failures all played out for him like a window directly into the past. He'd seen so much, yet he blanched at the idea of committing any of it to words.

Instead, he pulled the pack of smokes out from his back pocket. Gazing in, his face tightened and spirit sank at the way the remaining cigarettes bounced about and leaned haphazardly against one another.

Drawing a pair out, he handed one to Alex and returned the pack to his pocket. "I guess I've been seeing myself," he answered. "For a long time, before I died, I'd been operating under some pretty destructive delusions. I always acted like tomorrow was when I'd turn everything around and get back in control—tomorrow, that lauded day that's always just around the corner.

"I've been putting things off, like a master escape artist, and I guess I've finally escaped. I know I'll never complete BHI now, never get to show you guys the plans I had. I spent my whole life certain that things would end up just working out. But in the long run, they just ended.

"I still don't know how I died." Edgar gazed off into space as he spoke, and the wailing music and angel cheers were lost beneath the weight of his sad soliloquy. "Uncertainty, imbalance, loneliness, and a failed attempt at turning things around—that's all I've got now, and it's driving me mad.

"It would be so easy to say I just needed a bit more time, but that's what I've been saying for far too long. Now, I just want closure. I know what went wrong, it was nothing new…"

"Stop!" Chanel's high-pitched screech ended Edgar's eloquent insight. Behind them, a crowd of angels pounded desperately at the base of the bull, which jockeyed, bounced, and spun, turning the terrified Chanel into an ebony blur clinging desperately to its golden torso.

Finally, its reckless routine concluded, and again it settled back down into place as a shaken and sick Chanel poured off and stumbled haltingly away.

"What were you saying, Edgar? It sounds like you're really onto something." Emeric sucked slowly at the straw in his rum and coke.

Edgar blinked, working to rearrange the scattered mosaic of his thoughts as he inhaled from his cigarette, chasing it with a long swallow of brandy. "I really just waited too long. I remember so many nights out at The Scholar with you guys, laughing like jackals about the future and how the world would just open up for the lot of us. When we hang out now, we talk about those times, and I admit it's always nice to share a few laughs about the old days of guts and glory. But as I sit there smiling, I always find myself wondering where it all went wrong; how it all ended. I remember feeling like you'd all just found your own ways to give up the dream—that I was the only one holding true to course."

No one said a word. They didn't need to. Edgar's broad shoulders slumped, and his head sagged. Glancing up sadly, he found another dark shooter on the bar and snatched it up for himself. "For my unending avoidance and blind faith; my lack of vision and…oh, whatever. Fuck it…I do hereby supplicate myself." Edgar didn't even taste the shot. His mind was far away, and he fought for focus, habitually placing the empty shot glass in line with the rest.

Jake snorted. "Fuck this, Edgar, just say that word, bro."

"Calm down Jake, I deserve this." Edgar spoke through clenched teeth.

He could feel his shirt bunching up beneath his suit jacket, wet with sweat. "It's getting hot as…" Edgar avoided clichés whenever possible.

A sudden silence hijacked the atmosphere of the bar, causing the ring of friends to turn around nervously.

At the centre of the hall sat the golden bull. Dark plumes of smoke drifted from its gilded nostrils, and its red eyes shone. Two lines of angels flanked it, creating a tunnel of flesh leading up to the steps of the abysmal beast.

At the far end of the line stood Tyra. "Let me show you ladies how it's done," she cooed, peeling off her red silk dress.

Tyra stretched her thin arms out above her head, cracking her knuckles as she made an exaggerated display of swinging her hips from side to side. This resulted in a matching sway in her more than generous bosom.

"God damn, you know how to throw a party, Edgar. I can't believe you hit that!" Jake gushed.

Tyra strode down the line of angels, and the muscles playing beneath her tight skin were roadmaps to unspeakable satisfaction. Mounting the bull afforded a somewhat less graceful view, but the awestruck shine in Jake's eyes remained undiminished.

As the gears roared to life and the contraption began to turn, Tyra moaned in anticipation.

"So Edgar." Duncan arched his thick eyebrows and took a sip of scotch,

"What now?"

Lighting a fresh cigarette, Edgar considered the question. "Well, there isn't a whole lot left, really. I just need to figure out exactly what happened the Saturday of my death. Then hopefully I can make peace with the whole sordid affair that has been the life of Edgar Vincent."

"You'll excuse my asking," said Duncan, "but it occurs to me that you already know all the contributing factors. Is the exact cause of your death really that important?"

"It is actually, Duncan." A sharp edge was creeping into Edgar's voice. "I couldn't tell you why, but I'm sure I won't find peace until I know what happened. I know I've got my flaws, but still, I always believed things were going to be OK, that life had a way of working itself out. I just can't rest without knowing exactly how it all fell apart—how could I have ended up so scared and alone?"

He shuddered and continued only after several gulps from a fresh cup of brandy. "Jesus, I sound like a fucking ghost. Is this what happens after six days in the afterlife? Or has it been seven?" He was met only with blank stares and realized what a meaningless concept time was in a realm like this. A chill ran through his body, competing fiercely with the sweltering air of the ballroom for total dominance of his senses.

"Ooooh!" Tyra's yelp tore through the hall. A broad smile was smeared across her pretty face as she was tossed and twirled upon the back of the golden bull. "Aaaah!"

"So what are you going to do?" Alex asked.

"Keep going, I guess," Edgar replied absently. "I've seen what an ass I've been and learned what mistakes I've made. Thanks to you shits, I've even done my shots of contrition, but there's still no peace. I don't feel any different. Strange surroundings, horrible revelations, but through it all I'm still just me. Edgar. Isn't something supposed to change?"

"Well, accepting your faults is a good first step," Emeric offered hopefully.

"Yeah, but what's it gotten me? I still don't know how I was left alone down there or what the hell I might have done in those last minutes to wind up here. Without that payoff, without any answers, what's the fucking point?"

Now Duncan spoke. "I don't think "payoff" was ever the point of taking responsibility, Edgar. Besides, you're still fixating on the past, expecting the future to take care of itself."

"There is no future, Duncan. It's all over, remember?"

"Yet time goes on. And you need to as well," Duncan answered.

"Oh, fuck!" screamed Tyra. Her smooth, naked body spun and jostled, held in thrall to the mechanical beast locked between her firm thighs. Her eyes rolled in her head, and the smile on her lips threatened to split her face down the centre as her auburn hair cracked across her ivory back like a slave master's whip. "Oh God!"

"How am I supposed to go on when I don't even know where I'm going?" Edgar's fists were tight at his sides, and his low voice dripped with contempt.

"A bit late for that particular inquiry." Duncan's cool demeanour was pushing pins under the fingernails of Edgar's patience.

"Oh goddammit, Duncan! I'm aware you all knew better, I've seen the evidence, believe me. But all your precious wisdom and foresight does jack shit now. You probably told me a million times what was going to happen, and I'm happy for you—really. I know I was blind, I know it wasn't just you I lied to, but that doesn't make it any damn easier looking back, does it? It doesn't change anything."

"And it isn't meant to," Duncan continued, unmoved. For all his self-control and detached intellect, he'd always shared Edgar's headstrong fixation with making his point. "You are," he finished flatly.

"Oh, very helpful, Duncan, that's just what I need. What the fuck am I supposed to do with that?"

"Admit," said Duncan, and Edgar's heart raced as he saw the dark shooter Duncan held out under his icy gaze, "that the mistakes of the past, and the false hopes for the future, are irrelevant, and change. It's not so hard, Edgar. You have everything you need right here. Just accept it, embrace it, and move the fuck on."

Edgar stared at his friend, and the smoky breath from his nostrils was the exhaust of a machine engineered only to persist.

"Oh Christ!" Tyra's squeal was more pitched now, and her eyes were orbs of white as her back arched and her lips curled. "Oh Edgar!" she screamed, her knees knocking against the drum-like torso of the bull as her body convulsed like a dying engine.

Then the bull was done, and with a final hiss, it collapsed back down in a cloud of steam. Still trembling, Tyra slid exhausted from its saddle, and the unearthly smile etched upon her face was the only evidence of life.

To his surprise, the shooter was in Edgar's hand now. Jake gulped his beer in oblivious ecstasy as he stared at Tyra. Emeric just gazed at the ground, and Alex's glassy eyes were somewhere else entirely. But Duncan stood right before him, staring at him with unflinching determination.

"What the fuck are you looking for, Duncan?" Edgar demanded in a voice of vim and vitriol. His eyes ricocheted feverishly between Duncan and the shot in his own trembling hand.

Duncan smiled, the faultless composure of his countenance never faltering. "Look around you, Edgar. There's nothing left to fight for. You're here."

Slouching beside Edgar in a daze, Alex jolted upright, his eyes suddenly aglow. Gazing about in a wide arc, his mouth gaped as he spoke. "Holy shit you guys, he's right. Check this place out!"

Edgar understood. His pack of smokes bulged in his back pocket as he took a sip from his fine brandy. His best friends stood all around him, and beyond were more beautiful women than even he could imagine.

*Well...*Edgar fully perceived the irony.

So much on offer, yet all he could focus on was Duncan.

Duncan...

Edgar glared daggers into Duncan's puffed-out chest. His friend had been increasingly judgemental in life, but here in the afterlife, his sole purpose seemed to be bringing him down and second-guessing all he did. Now he stood before Edgar, tall and proud. His ridiculous red tie waved from side to side of its own volition, and his smile curled into pitchfork points. He wanted real accountability, and Edgar's blood ran cold. He insisted on Edgar accepting himself—not with plans or reflections—but active efforts. Edgar's feet itched for movement. He knew that above all, Duncan wanted him to accept the moment and be himself rather than simply talking about who that might be.

Edgar fought to find the words, but none came. The shooter was heavy as he raised it up. He imagined just being in the moment; no plans for change, no excuses for folly.

The shooter was an anvil as he raised it toward his lips.

Still, Duncan watched attentively; so too did Emeric, Alex, and Jake. The shooter hovered before Edgar's mouth for a moment as he considered giving up the fight and standing as an unafflicted equal in the company of his peers. He stared back into the even, expectant eyes of his oldest friend. Then with a rush, he brought the shooter down hard.

"Mother—"

*****

Best intentions had never done a goddamn thing for Edgar. It always came down to action.

Standing across from Duncan in the stony silence of the Golden Ballroom, Edgar reached for a cigarette. "Fuck this," he mumbled as he sparked it to life. He could see his tired face reflected in the silver of his lighter. "We should head somewhere with a bit more life."

"Yeah!" Jake joined enthusiastically. But his gaze darted between Edgar and the bull, and his face was a mask of uncertainty.

Alex took it all in, his mouth wide open yet unspeaking.

"What do you mean, Edgar?" asked Emeric, pushing his glasses up to meet his eyes—shimmering with doubt.

"I came here to make amends, and I've done that," Edgar's words came slow and dry. "But I also came to start something new—to be my best self and to start finding some peace in what's left of my fucking existence.

"But I can't really do that with this asshole constantly trying to bring me down. I'm trying to improve myself; I even did the shots in good humour. But it's never enough for Duncan."

"Best self?" Duncan repeated incredulously.

"Yes, dammit," Edgar's voice cracked as he spoke, and its pace gained speed like rainwater flowing downhill. "But I can't really achieve that when I'm surrounded by nothing but negativity."

Duncan ignored his bait—a professional through and through. "Who is that, Edgar? Who are you going to be?"

"Me, Duncan, myself—your friend, if you don't recall. I know I've made mistakes, and I've tried to make up for that. But I'm not going to suffer for them forever."

"Hell no! Not in the afterlife!" Jake cheered, rejoining the conversation with no hint of irony. The crowd was dispersing now, and there was nothing more to see at the golden bull.

"I'm ready to go. I've said what I came here to say, and learned what I needed to. Jake's right, it's time I find something to make me feel alive."

"But Edgar," Emeric spoke in a wavering whimper, "this is where we are."

"I'm sorry, Emmy, and I do think you should come. But if I'm going to spend eternity surrounded by whatever I imagine, I'm going to make the most of it, dammit."

"You're going to run, Edgar. Just like always." It wasn't spite in Duncan's tone. Edgar couldn't place it, but it certainly wasn't the condescension he was expecting—which struck him as especially odd given what he now knew of the afterlife.

"Call it what you want, Duncan, but I'm done with pity and regret. I may be dead, but I'm not done living yet. Who's coming with me?"

Emeric gazed down forlornly.

Alex gaped, slowly shaking his head.

Duncan just stared—cold and unaffected.

"Fuck yeah, I am!" cried Jake as he fell into step behind Edgar, who tugged dejectedly at the flimsy collar of his suit jacket and turned in a hurried retreat. Past wilting balloons and trampled streamers, he marched. The golden bull sat lifeless as he brushed by, and his friends watched his departure sadly. "Whooo!" An enthusiastic cry was taken up, and a small army of angels closed in around Edgar. Tall girls whose proportions spit in the face of earthly physics, women in gowns so elegant that royalty might blush in shame, and others so unadorned that even the most lecherous soul might do the same.

Jasmine was there, and Leslie. Tiffany—seemingly recovered and back in the positive spirits of a kitten on meth—strutted happily alongside Chanel, whose striped dress flowed luxuriously behind her. At their head was Tyra, her shimmering scarlet outfit tossed ineffectually over one shoulder.

Gold was everywhere, yet still, Edgar could see no trace of the Silver Angel. There was no comfort here. His friends had turned against him, and his grand hopes for redemption lay now in ruins.

"I'm not so sure this is heaven…"

Jake followed dutifully behind, happy and boisterous as he walked among the angels towards the hedonism and debauchery he'd adored ever since Edgar had welcomed him into its warm embrace.

The double doors of the Golden Ballroom were tall and heavy, gilded and carved with detailed reliefs which at any other moment would have brought a sentimental smile to Edgar's handsome face.

They opened of their own volition, revealing the thick grey fog without. Behind him, the vaulted ceiling, the booze, and the Golden Ballroom faded. Edgar's few remaining friends watched in regretful silence as he heaved a contented sigh and marched away from it all, disappearing into the murky fog like a long overdue homecoming.

CHAPTER 9
THE BLOODY ALLEY

No matter the deplorable circumstances Edgar managed to get himself into, he'd always maintained an impressive ability to find the silver lining. No fallout with a woman had ever derailed his steadfast determination, nor left him with anything less than a throbbing headache and a strengthened resolve to troll the depths for better fish in the figurative sea.

His long history of agonizing Sunday mornings had never diminished his passion for the preceding Saturdays; a quick check for missing belongings and regretful phone calls always sufficed to put Edgar back in motion and set his path towards the next inevitable night of debauchery.

Indeed, the endless trail of chaos and calamity which followed in Edgar's wake had historically served as little more than an increased impetus to seek greener pastures, and it was difficult for anyone who knew him to deny that, with an apathetic shrug and optimistic smile, Edgar was certain to find them, violate them, and leave them barren as he blazed recklessly on.

Once, Edgar had been released from a very promising job scoring for a short feature film. The dismissal came not as a result of his frequent absences and occasional on-set dalliances, but rather was the product of his reaction to an admittedly mild tongue-lashing from the producer. Edgar spent an entire night splicing together recordings of the producer, taking a word here and a phrase there to create an embarrassing, Frankenstein-monster confession of sound bites. He'd then left it playing on loop, forcing the bewildered morning staff to listen to it incessantly as they arrived for their day's work.

As he'd left the studio with his belongings in a duffle bag later that day, Edgar had felt it was a personal low point.

Of course, that was many personal low points ago.

Following a quick bender, he had rationalized that the project hadn't been right for him after all.

At any rate, he had little trouble finding a more suitable position. The director of a small-budget infomercial, in need of an affordable composer, was a well-known drunkard and womanizer. He and Edgar forged a strong bond as the project moved forward, until a disagreement over "claiming rights" managed to spoil that relationship as well. But infomercials had never really been a passion for Edgar anyway.

Unaffected, unrepentant, and undeterred, he was a veritable model of resilience. Yes, the situation had to be dire indeed to throw old Edgar off—and dire it was.

The cracking apart of his sticky eyelids coupled with the resulting influx of glaring light sent sirens of protest across the battlefield in his skull. A shocked cry of pain revealed a desert in his mouth—a fire in his lungs. His entire body ached, and his stomach roiled. The inside of his throat was lined with barbed wire, and his blood ran slow and cold through his brittle limbs.

Edgar awoke with a start, suddenly aware of the unmistakable weight of a dainty arm clasping him in its peaceful slumber.

Still here on Sunday? he wondered woefully. Edgar didn't know the half of it.

His dry teeth tasted like old whiskey and stale cigarettes, and the entire room stank of sweat. From somewhere in the distance came the slow rise of beating drums, accompanied by what might have been a mandolin.

Thud. Thud.

Edgar was reasonably sure the tune was one of his own. The notion struck him as odd, but with his head spinning and a terrible ache in his guts, he couldn't begin to sort it out.

Time for a tactful extrication, he determined.

Falling instinctually into habits long since ingrained into muscle memory with the precision of a well-practiced dancer, Edgar lifted the thin appendage barely an inch and began to squirm out from under. Supporting the limp arm with one hand, he combined the efforts of his opposite elbow with small movements of his hips to begin the careful retreat from this Sunday's heartless impositions.

Thud. Thud.

What the hell did I do to my abs? he wondered, grimacing with pain before rolling his eyes and accepting the increased suffering necessary to mute a self-conscious chuckle.

Continuing his slow extraction, he was startled by a sudden giggle from his right that sent hot, grenadine-scented gusts of breath searing across his tired face.

It took no time for Edgar to realize his situation was more difficult than he'd initially thought.

Squinting against the invasive light, he barely managed to discern the outline of a pigtail jutting up from the shaking, chortling form beside him.

Tiffany, he realized with a shameful grimace. But the arm still in his hand stretched off in the opposite direction, and with a slow turn of his head, he distinguished Tyra's long auburn hair strewn across his fresh white pillows. Suddenly, the unnerving implication behind his own music being on struck home.

Thud. Thud. Boom!

At my own house to boot? Dammit, Edgar!

No matter—Edgar was no rank amateur. Adjusting his exit strategy on the fly, he raised Tyra's arm an inch further and, with the joint effort of his elbow and ass, began inching down towards the bottom of the bed.

The startling sensation of his toes sinking into the fatty excess of a large breast proved enough to kill any lingering hope for a subtle exit.

"Goddammit!" he bellowed, again changing tactics like the vet he certainly was.

Thud. Thud. Slam!

A sudden flurry of motion caused the bed to jump and heave like a freshly branded bull. In the scorching morning light, Edgar sank despondently back into the mattress and watched as Tiffany and Tyra, Chanel and two unfamiliar angels made a hasty retreat in a brilliant display of flesh, which would have prompted a less experienced man to snap a quick mental image.

"That's more like it," Edgar rasped, his raw throat straining with the effort.

Peeling himself up from his bed of sin, he took quick account of his room. A lamp in the corner was tipped over, and the floor might as well have been a graveyard for albino snakes with all the condoms strewn about. The room's corners were piled with undergarments, and he noticed the empty frame of a mirror leaning atop the headboard as he grabbed a fresh pair of jeans and an undershirt from his closet.

Pulling them on, he stepped carefully around the shattered glass of the actual mirror near the door and shook his head with a resigned laugh as he left his room and started down the hallway. Earrings, empty bottles, and twisted thongs were strewn along its booze-reeking length. He had no idea the whereabouts of his phone, but his current mood didn't leave him particularly inclined to place his celebratory call to Emmy anyways—even if his present circumstances assured him it would be entirely justified.

Turning into his study, he watched as the last few angels scattered out the front door. Leslie held a pillow to her chest as she fled bare-assed down the hall, while Jasmine strode out with all the poise and grace that could be afforded a nude woman in her present circumstances.

Following the sound of his music, Edgar found an old battery-operated stereo lying on the floor. Thud. Thud…crack! He slapped the power button with a dismissive shake of his spinning head.

He smiled. *That's the end of that.* However, a quick glance around his study told him this was far from the case.

The instruments formerly lining his walls were now littered carelessly about the apartment—strings broken and levers bent. His prized Telecaster guitar was a steampunk cactus rising from a pot of dirt; the plant previously inhabiting the pot lay like a dead squid on the ground beside it, bereft of leaves.

"He loves me, he loves me not," Tyra's tuneless song echoed through his mind as the fiasco that was his home assembled into a blurry mosaic of the preceding night's ill-advised decisions.

His synthesizer was soaked, his mixing-station mangled, and speakers of all shapes and sizes were scattered about in a sordid state of disrepair. Half-finished drinks were set out upon his keyboard, his bar was utterly empty, and cigarette burns dotted the sticky surface of his cherished old desk.

Indeed, there appeared to be only one survivor. Resting on a loveseat in the far corner of his study, swaddled in a blanket Edgar didn't recall owning, sat his fucking keytar. Torn leaves were braided into its shoulder-strap.

"Bye baby bunting." The strange audio memory was Tiffany this time. Edgar shook his head, a flat chuckle rumbling up his aching throat as he took in the depths of destruction.

"What the fuck happened?" he wondered aloud, his fingers tracing slow circles around his temples.

"Beats me, broseph! But I'll never forget the sight of those fine ladies leaving!" Jake's giant hand clapped into Edgar's back, very nearly causing his night's indulgences to spill over the floor of his study.

Jake was leaning against the couch, slumped over and exhausted. His eyes were red, his cheeks were sunken, and he wore only a towel.

Stumbling over to a crinkled pile of black fabric pushed against his desk, Edgar recognized his crushed suit-jacket with a barely subdued grin. A quick

touch told him it was soaked, and a follow-up sniff pinned down the culprit—
gin. His stomach turned over in proactive protest.

The shattered glass of a pipe sat neatly gathered amidst the burn marks
on his desk, but upon the chair his leather jacket hung unharmed, bringing a
relieved smile to his haggard face. "Where did we go after the gala?"

"Can't say," Jake answered groggily. "I only know where we ended up."

As his hands slowly returned to his pulsing temples, Edgar concluded
that he'd set a new precedent for god-awful hangovers. "I don't remember a
fucking thing."

It wasn't strictly true. He did remember the gala: the lilting balloons, the
tattered streamers, and the great golden bull. He recalled the argument he'd
had, and he remembered...

"Duncan. I ran from Duncan."

"So, what now?" asked Jake.

"I don't know." Edgar absently shuffled some broken glass across the
wooden floor with his bare foot. "I think I was onto something last night;
like I was beginning to put it all together..." He moved slowly across the
room as he spoke, circling around his desk and opening the bottom right
drawer, careful to avoid making even the slightest noise. Inside, the bottle of
celebratory scotch reserved for the completion of BHI sat untouched. His
tattered old tie lay haphazardly beside it. By all evidence, the scotch was the
only alcohol which had made it through the night. *The last man standing in a
once-crowded arena,* he thought with a silly smirk on his face and a queer feeling
in his gut.

Shoving the drawer shut and circling back towards Jake, he sighed. Then,
pulling a smoke from a pack he found on the couch and sparking it to life with
a lighter from the floor, finally concluded, "I'd been reflecting on something...
damned if I can recall what it was now, though."

"You know what that means?" asked Jake, a wry smile creeping out from
beneath his pained countenance.

Edgar's body groaned as he stared shakily at his well-weathered friend.
Considering a moment, he came up empty and raised an inquisitive eyebrow
in the big man's direction.

"It means this adventure ain't done yet," Jake stated matter-of-factly,
nodding curtly towards the door.

Edgar glanced around with an aching head and scorching throat. The
wreckage of his apartment was a potent, albeit familiar, harbinger that

something needed to change. He knew he needed to find direction—to transition from the desolation surrounding him into the greener pastures beyond.

"Hair of the dog," he affirmed, reaching for his jacket with a cavalier grin.

*****

The bar was a trashy sort of place—just the type of dive Edgar used to retreat to when he felt the need to push aside his sorrows and focus on the happier things in life. It was a place to unwind and seek comfort, a seedy little corner of nowhere free of judgment, where he could safely assume that most of the other patrons were at least as bad off as he was.

It wasn't the first one they'd been to. After passing through his front door into the expected fog without, he and Jake had visited a dozen just like it.

Flashes of neon lights and the clank of dull brown beer bottles formed an ineffectual roadmap of their bender. It had seen the increasingly inebriated duo through the musty alleys and brightly lit streets of a city-scape that perched ever on the distant side of familiar.

With each new bar had come new starting shots, new angels, and old conversations. They sat now on tall black barstools, sipping their beers in pensive silence as they watched a menagerie of angels flit about on the checkerboard dance floor to their left.

It was the dance floor that stood out the most to Edgar, but no matter the effort he exerted in racking his memory for a name, in the end, he'd fallen short. He harboured vague recollections of the place and was relatively certain he'd been there at some point in life with Duncan.

Desperate times indeed. Edgar shook his head moodily. If he'd been here with Duncan, he must have been in a truly sorry state. Although his oldest friend, Duncan's success had gone to his head to an unbearable degree, and Edgar only opened up to him now in dire need. More often he relied on the company of Jake, whose judgment was non-existent, even if his interests were somewhat linear.

"Check out that one!" Jake broke the silent screen of Edgar's sullen reflections, his beefy hand stretching across the table to indicate a Latina angel wearing pink velour pants and a low-cut rhinestone top. She ground sensually to the heavy bass loops, shaking her posterior in a mirror image of Tyra, who danced behind her.

"C'mon Edgar, tell me something Spanish to say," Jake pleaded; failing utterly to conceal his giddy anticipation as he once again set a trap he was certain his despondent friend would finally fall for.

"Fuck you, Jake," Edgar answered curtly, his strong jaw resting in a shaking palm. With each beer he'd consumed—a copious number to be sure—he'd only slipped further into his own sinister reflections. Imbalance and towers, isolation and the uncertainty of turning around. And Duncan—the endless posturing and insistences. *As if he knew my life better than I did.*

"Can you believe his nerve?" he asked around the lip of his beer.

"Who, buddy? We're the only dudes here." Jake was confused. It was by no means an unusual state for Jake, but it had been even more common this night, as Edgar continually trailed off into seemingly unrelated mumblings and long strings of expletives.

Jake wasn't wrong, however; aside from themselves, the bar was filled solely with angels. "Isn't that the point?" Jake finished, an uncertain sneer gnarling up his heavily stubbled cheeks.

"Duncan, you idiot—trying to tell me how to live my afterlife. What's he trying to achieve? I'm already dead, and as events have clearly proven, I can't get any deader.

"What I can do is use my situation to find a bit of fucking satisfaction. Is that really too much to ask?"

Jake frowned, tacitly realizing that even he should have known who Edgar was referring to at this point. "You're right, man, Duncan's an asshole." Jake pulled a cigarette from the open pack Edgar had left in the middle of the table and fired it up. One of the benefits of death the two men had agreed on over the course of their binge was that the rules of polite society were no longer in effect.

That, and the imperative ability to adapt their surroundings to Edgar's own expectations.

…And the angels. Jake seemed to appreciate the angels more than all the other benefits combined. "Don't let him get you down." Jake stared over with a satisfied smile, eager to believe his sage advice would put an end to Edgar's dark fixation.

"It's not even about change," Edgar interjected between puffs of his own smoke, proving Jake's hopes fruitless. "It's just that considering the fucking circumstances, it's kind of nice to feel alive." He waved a hand, and a waif-like waitress sped by, depositing a large tray of assorted shots and beers on the table. Both men eagerly helped themselves.

A sudden cheer was taken up on the dance floor, and Jake beamed as he watched Tyra gyrating atop a speaker stack. Below her, Tiffany had managed to uncork a bottle of champagne. The infamous foamy spray had eluded her, however, and she shook it now in a haphazard effort to compensate, sending large puddles splashing onto the floor and the occasional burst splattering over her thin face. This sight only caused Jake's enthusiasm to grow, threatening to split his smile in two before he finally managed to pull free of the siren's trance and return his attention to his maligned friend.

"I'm with you, Edgar. The way I see it, I could sit alone at home and read a book or something—"

"Definitely 'or something,'" Edgar interrupted with a snarky grin.

Jake huffed. "Whatever."

"A comic, maybe."

"Fuck you! A comic then," Jake conceded petulantly. "Anyway, I could sit and do that every night, and I'd live to be old and lonely. Well maybe I can't avoid getting old or being miserable, but at least I can try to avoid the double whammy."

Edgar smoked in contemplative silence. Jake had taken the words right out of his mouth. *I wonder why Duncan was so insistent anyway.*

"Hey sweetie, why don't you read between the lines?" Leslie bent over the table, a tall shot glass full of clear liquor held snugly between her ocher breasts.

"Try that guy." Edgar brushed her off. "It's the only reading he'll do all year."

Jake beamed, the pleasure of the act far-outweighing the sting of the insult.

Edgar shook his head, washing the thoughts from it with a long swallow of beer. He knew he shouldn't be so hard on Jake, but the potential for comedy was just so ripe with the big lout. As a matter of fact, at Edgar's urging, Jake had once made a three-month, 10-page foray into writing. Edgar thought it would broaden Jake's mind, thus making him a more balanced drinking partner. The novel never worked out, but Edgar remained mildly impressed with Jake's chosen title, although he doubted his dough-headed friend fully comprehended how apt *Titular* was, given the subject matter.

"So, dude," Jake said with a devilish grin after finishing his shot. "We gonna scoop up some of these angels or what?"

I might as well be alone, for all the company this imbecile provides. Edgar finished his smoke, lit another, and pulled hard.

...Just like the night of my death.

The thought sent a shiver up his spine, which he answered with a long swallow of beer. As the rest of the inner circle grew up and moved on with their lives, Jake alone had remained steadfast in his support of Edgar's more hedonistic desires. That meant a great deal to Edgar. Although Jake didn't make for the most stimulating company, Edgar had long since learned that going out alone—when not seeking immediate female company at least—was never a good idea.

Staring off quietly, puffing on his smoke, he remembered walking home one night—alone, lost, and impossibly inebriated. Stumbling from one end of the sidewalk to the other and back, he'd proceeded slowly, singing a barely recognizable rendition of *Sympathy for the Devil.*

He hadn't planned to go out that night at all. The original plan had been to spend the night alone in his study, enjoying a fine bottle of rye while putting in some serious hours on the BHI score. But his efforts were met with little reward, and after only a few hours work, he'd given up the ghost of his high-minded ambitions, and quickly concluded it would be far more beneficial to do some "field research."

With such short notice, even Jake hadn't been available. But the tenacious Edgar was undeterred and headed out alone to find out just how basically indecent a human could be.

He'd set new records, he was quite sure, but as he'd finished up his tune and stumbled blindly across the street in the early dawn, he'd shamefully realized he had no chance of remembering exactly how, which rendered his putting off work on BHI entirely unjustified. *There's always next time*, he'd chuckled to himself, working feverishly to rub a large spot of dirt off his old leather jacket.

Putting BHI off had become something of a trend by that point. Every time Edgar endeavoured to make headway on his definitive work, some cruel distraction arose, presenting a new effigy to blame for his failures, and all his fine intentions were inevitably pushed off into the promising embrace of "tomorrow."

And so he'd walked, working in vain to spark his dead lighter to life as his tongue ran tiny circles around the gap formerly occupied by his tooth.

Edgar didn't have any recollection of how he'd lost it; he'd just known that it was gone. It had been among the first things he'd checked for after being thrown out of the last open bar, yet only the second biggest disappointment of the night. *Going out alone is one thing—going home alone is just a fucking embarrassment.*

Nonetheless, the lesson was at least partially learned, and ever afterward Edgar did all he could to arrange company whenever he decided to truly tie one on.

Even if the company is less than ideal...

Now, Jake leaned over the table, inserting his thick skull imploringly into Edgar's line of sight. "Edgar, dude, what do you say? Let's pick up some angels—maybe even remember it this time?"

Edgar wasn't inclined to remember a goddamn thing. With a lazy turn of his head, he took in the angels on offer.

Tyra still swayed back and forth to the thudding beats emanating from the speakers beneath her delicate feet—her legs bowed to the point of negating even the most abstract purpose of her short red skirt.

Leslie and Jasmine bobbed together on the edge of the dance floor, their heaving breasts bouncing to the rhythm as Chanel shook her hips and took in the others with a keen, shining eye.

Tiffany spun her lithe form tunelessly through the crowd, shaking her ass as if for Edgar's eyes alone.

The entire bar was a veritable shrine of flesh and fantasy, and Edgar flicked his cigarette between two yellowed fingers, watching it all.

I was alone, he reflected morosely.

To his right, the city shone through a window plastered with ads for expensive drinks and instant gratification. The scene outside was eerily familiar.

I tried to turn around, he obsessed.

There was a cold beer in his hand, beautiful women were all around, and Jake watched him intently, ever eager for input and guidance.

"How did I end up here?" Edgar ruminated aloud.

"In heaven?" Jake mumbled the clarification around the beer bottle in his mouth.

Edgar tossed his dying smoke away over his shoulder. Reaching for another, he played around with two fingers, struggling to find one in the increasingly desolate pack. He ignored Jake's question.

"How could I have been alone?" he asked. A haphazard roll of his head transformed the bar into a psychedelic blur of flashing lights and dark spaces. "Where was everyone else?"

"Who could ever keep up with you, Edgar?" Jake clapped him on the back as he spoke, his face a bewildering mask of envy and consternation.

"And yet they're here to judge me? How the hell does that work? If they couldn't understand where I was coming from in life, what fucking right do they have now?"

"Exactly!" Jake boomed his support, pounding his beer into the table before slamming its remnants down his throat with an appreciative belch.

"I never thought I was better than anyone Jake, don't mistake it for that. It was just a matter of priorities. Duncan talks about his pension plans and net worth, and I just think it's nonsense. He's not going to retire at 55 and think about all those clever savings he made. He'll wonder what he might have done with the time he had."

Jake stared blankly at Edgar.

"Are you really just going to sit there talking all night?" Chanel purred into Edgar's ear, holding her hands out as she backed towards the dance floor, encouraging him to stand up and join her.

Edgar dismissed her with a quick shake of his head. "He's trapped himself in a job he barely enjoys and has no time to see the people he actually cares about. Sure he's got a beautiful home, but he hardly gets to spend a waking moment in it. He's got an enormous bank account with nothing to buy, and when he eventually finds some poor idiot to settle down with, he'll probably be too exhausted every night to enjoy any of it. What kind of life is that?

"And don't get me wrong, Jake," Edgar continued, uninterested in any answer Jake might have come up with. "I wanted those things too. You know I'd have loved to meet a respectable woman and make her mine, and I definitely wanted to have a few kids of my own someday; little Edgars to carry on the tradition, you know. I just wanted to be able to live a bit along the way, instead of just staying alive."

Jake nodded, then furrowed his brow as he gazed about the environs of the bar, "…respectable woman?"

"I had it once," Edgar stated flatly. "And as for money and direction, that's what BHI was about. I was getting things together dammit, and on my own terms!"

"BHI, your book, right?"

Edgar sighed. "It was the documentary I was scoring, Jake, you know this. *Basic Human Indecency*—it was about the things people take for granted, and how easily distracted the majority of humanity is by shallow shit like money and status. It's exactly what I'm saying! People never appreciate the time they have. But that's all I ever wanted to do!"

Something about the conversation struck Edgar as entirely too familiar, and he self-consciously pulled the collar of his jacket snugly against his neck. It took another two shots from the supply on the table to silence the nagging understanding gestating in the deep recesses of his weary brain.

"That's what Duncan couldn't understand. None of them could."

"You're still fixating on the past, expecting the future to take care of itself." The memory of Duncan's voice painted Edgar's vision red, and he finished his beer quickly to chase it from his mind. Beside him, Tiffany continued to shake her ass in a dance which looked less like a physical complement to the music than a shaky child's attempt to tie her shoes.

"Fuck this!" Edgar's conviction boiled up through clenched teeth. "Fuck Bev, fuck Emeric, fuck BHI, and fuck Duncan!"

Jake surged forward with a devilish grin, "Yeah, dude! You've fucked everything that's come across your path! Hell—isn't that why we're here?"

Jake held his soup-bone fist out for a confirmatory bump, but Edgar only gaped.

Then he moved.

The crack of Tiffany's empty skull bouncing off the dance floor drew the attention of the entire bar as Edgar pocketed his smokes and elbowed her aside on his way to the door.

Only the sound of Jake's braying laughter followed him outside. Edgar hit the street running, a terrible familiarity tearing at his conscience like the claws of demons on his back.

His fists clenched and his arms pumped as he ran alone through bright streets and bleak alleys, his teeth grating like old stones.

Jake's laughter continued to echo between the tall buildings, buffeting Edgar with volley after volley of taunting torment.

But it wasn't Jake he was running from.

His legs churned like pistons, and Edgar thought solely of the disappointment in Duncan's eyes as he'd turned away from his childhood friend.

One of the more common expressions I've seen, he acknowledged, but the wry observation did nothing to lighten his dark mood.

"Just accept it, embrace it, and move the fuck on," Duncan's voice penetrated his being.

"Move on to what? Where the fuck am I supposed to be going?" he screamed, but the bustling city streets offered no consolation. Edgar was tired of running but afraid of what lay behind him. He needed to escape, but booze and women promised none of the comforts they used to.

Why is this happening to me? What did I do to deserve this? What the hell am I meant to be doing?

Turning blindly from one alley to the next, he felt his steps guided by some inaccessible memory. A heavy cloak of foreboding settled over him and threatened suffocation when he noticed a great tower rising above the hazy streets in the distance.

A sinking feeling in his gut served only to confirm his path.

Gruesome gargoyles jutted from the corners of the tower at even intervals along its height, and upon its peak perched the familiar cross which had so often acted as the lighthouse to Edgar's wayward childhood odysseys.

"Without faith Edito, a man is just a man. And what is that, after all?" The high voice of his Nana came amid the screeching tires and honking horns of the restless city, and the chilling answer could not have been more apparent to Edgar Vincent.

Shaking his head as he wove through dark streets, he fought savagely to escape the understanding he felt grasping at his coat-tails from the shadows. The few remaining cigarettes in his packet rattled with each frenzied step, pounding out a marching beat for his desperate flight.

How do I stop this? What do I need to do? Sweat stung his eyes, and his body cramped and spasmed under the strain of his escape.

"You're going to run Edgar, just like always." Bile rose in Edgar's throat as Duncan's voice sounded in his ear with all the subtlety of scraping blades.

Shit. Edgar had no doubt now. *This was the night!*

It hadn't been Jake. He was just a proxy. Edgar had been out with Duncan, sitting in some trashy bar on a lonely Saturday night, unloading his fears on the one man whose opinion he actually valued. But it was too much for him, and he'd turned away from wisdom, back to the old certainty that with a bit of faith, everything else would be OK.

There were footsteps behind him now, and Edgar redoubled his efforts. His throat worked like a steam engine, yet still it failed to swallow the self-aware lump which had taken up residence within.

He was right, I did always run—I still am. The realization flooded Edgar's exhausted and abused mind. But each step brought the church tower closer—until it loomed over him like the beginning and end of all he ever was.

That's why I was alone, he understood. He'd run from help, from friends and sound advice. He'd fled again from what he needed into the embrace of what he knew.

Just like always.

The clatter of his drunken steps ricocheted between the cement walls to either side, and with a stumble, Edgar poured out of the alley into a broad courtyard.

The dark, disorienting fog pressed in from three sides, shutting off left and right, and denying exit the way he'd come. From the alley behind him, Edgar could still discern the sound of pursuing footsteps, but his attention was locked firmly ahead.

The church tower tore up into the dusky sky—separated from him by a long chain-link fence stretching off into the fog on either side.

A shiver ran up Edgar's spine, and his jaw hung silently agape. The top of the fence was coiled with barbed wire like serpents in wait and, of all the opportunities that had been afforded to him, it was here that Edgar finally found himself.

From the centre of the barbed wire, Edgar Vincent hung cold and lifeless.

Both arms of his jacket had gotten snagged on the spikes, stretching them out to his sides. A coil had looped about his neck, opening his throat and spilling his life's blood down over his white undershirt.

Doubling over and fighting to catch his breath, Edgar stumbled forward as small beads of blood splattered down and lay steaming on the hot cement. The courtyard was sweltering, and standing upright, he noticed that his own jacket now mirrored that of his corpse—torn and blood-soaked.

The pieces fell together quickly. After he'd fled from Duncan, he'd run towards the church, hoping to find a less cynical ear to unload his worries on. In his impassioned stupor, he'd attempted to scale the fence. But somewhere near the top he'd realized the stupidity of the goal. When he tried to turn around it all went wrong. He lost his footing—a sudden sense of imbalance—then overwhelming terror. He hung now, limp and still, a bloody crucifix dangling atop the rickety old fence. The tall church tower rose in outline above him, black against the crimson sky.

Behind him, the footsteps continued, but Edgar just stared straight ahead. *It would have made for a half-funny story,* he mused absently, *if only it had a brighter ending.*

Blood continued to rain down from his torn jacket, splashing onto the dried pool beneath his stiff body. There had been nothing heroic about his death, nothing to merit entrance into heaven. *But I'm well past that delusion by now,* he admitted in the furnace-like heat of the alley.

He drew a cigarette meekly from his pack. The dim light of the courtyard gained a flickering quality, and behind him, the approaching footsteps drew up and went silent. His heart skipped a beat, and he tucked the smoke behind his ear as he turned to face his pursuer.

Duncan's long, black pea coat was thrown open, and his green silk button-up shirt hung untucked from his dark slacks. Panting, he folded over and put his hands on his knees as he gazed up at Edgar—past and present.

"I tried to follow you, Edgar." Duncan's apologetic tone came between breathless rasps, and his eyes shimmered with regret. "I chased after you for so long, but I just couldn't keep up. You were too far gone."

Edgar opened his mouth, but no words came. From the fog behind Duncan appeared four tiny points of flame; candles held in the trembling hands of Edgar's lifelong friends.

Alex and Emeric, Jake, and even Bev. They stood holding little-cupped candles, their downcast eyes glinting in the unsteady light of their solemn vigil. *Some crazy fucking prank,* Edgar reasoned desperately. But he'd thought that before, and had already learned that he couldn't explain his way out of the nightmare his life had ended up.

"How could this happen to me? Where were you?" asked Edgar.

"We were out for drinks—we'd been talking about life, about your direction. You ran off. Edgar, I didn't mean to upset you, I just…" Duncan trailed off, his glassy eyes straining to impart sincerity where words failed.

Alex stepped forward, candle in hand. "I know it's not easy man, trust me. No one knows when they're gonna go. You've just gotta appreciate the times you had."

Disbelief choked Edgar's words. "The times I had?" he repeated incredulously. "That's pretty easy for you to say. You got out while things were still halfway decent. Do you have any clue how shitty it's gotten since then? The inner circle's all fallen apart, Alex, you have no idea!" He pulled a smoke from his packet and lit it up, sadly shaking his head.

Jake pouted. Emeric just stuttered, his eyes on the ground. Then, looking up with sudden determination, he stepped toward Edgar. "What do you mean? We all tried to be there for you."

"Be there for me? Really? How often have you been out lately, Emeric?" Edgar's face flushed as he spoke. "You're off with your own life, you don't have time for me. Jake's the only one who's been around with any consistency. But, I mean…that's Jake."

Jake smiled, missing Edgar's dismissive implication entirely.

"Edgar, we all tried. We did. You're not…"

"Shut up," Edgar cut Emeric off, his frustration mounting as he remembered bitterly that these 'friends' were mere projections of his own expectations of them. "What do you know?"

Duncan cracked his neck, harnessing his patience before stepping forward. "Edgar, you have to know…"

"And what about you?" Edgar ignored Duncan, wheeling around to face Bev. She stood quietly in her silver gown, just as he'd seen her in the Golden Ballroom. It seemed like a lifetime ago.

"Why are you even here?" he demanded, his muscles tensing like chain over a winch. "You left me flat out. You never believed in me. Sure, things get hard sometimes. You've got to struggle to get the good out of life—but you couldn't hack it. You never believed. You just never had any…"

Edgar bit his lip. Bev remained silent, her pretty face never reacting to the sting of his sharp words. "You've got to have faith," he finished feebly, staring at the totem of long-lost ideals standing before him.

Still, Bev said nothing. From the shining surface of her dress, Edgar's wild eyes gazed back at him. They were sunken and wet, darting feverishly about for something or someone to blame. He saw the cruel snarl of his mouth—vicious and beast-like. But beneath this, his lip quivered along with the uncertain convictions upon which he'd nailed his final hopes. "Faith…" he repeated impotently, finally understanding Bev's inscrutable silence. *I can't even imagine her having anything left to say.*

"Fuck this!" he wailed. "Fuck you all. I might as well be alone if this is the alternative. 'Friends' my ass," he spat, "I'm better off."

Jake nodded his indignant support.

Bev bowed her head sadly, stepping back with sloped shoulders and wet cheeks.

Alex knit his eyebrows together, staring doubtfully at Edgar, still struggling to conceive how his passionate ideals had led him so far astray.

Emeric shook his head, glaring in disgust. He opened his mouth briefly, as if to impart some final plea for decency, but closed it forlornly, finally resolving to accept the truth about Edgar.

For a moment longer the three friends stood in the heat of the alley, staring at Edgar from worlds away. Then they slowly backed into the fog, their perceived utility utterly exhausted in Edgar's defeated mind. Their candles flickered briefly through the fog, then sputtered out entirely.

Edgar took a long draw from his cigarette before glaring up at Duncan through eyes that were icy slits. "You always thought you had the answers, like you were the prototype for a life well-lived. What about your life, Duncan? You're just as much a slave to your choices as I am to mine. Where's your wife? Your kids? Oh yeah, Duncan, you rule the world all right, with your fancy little condo and 12-hour workdays. You really nailed it, man." Smoke billowed from his mouth as he spoke, rising farther up into the red sky with each hateful word.

Duncan bit his lip, turning away for a moment before meeting his friend's hard gaze. "At least I know where I'm going, Edgar. I'm actually trying to work towards something. Can you even tell me what you want any more?"

"A goddamn drink would be nice. A blowjob if we're being ambitious!" Edgar lit another smoke, turning his back dismissively to Duncan.

"You're wasting our fucking time, Edgar!" Duncan bellowed.

Jake shifted his weight from leg to leg uncomfortably, his focus following the argument along its course as he clenched his big, square jaw in confounded silence.

"I am? What are you even doing here, Duncan? Why bother if your time is so damn precious? All I've ever asked is that you have a bit of faith in me, let me make my own fucking decisions. It's not such a tall order!" Edgar stared nails through his old friend, and saw through years gone by the young man he'd grown up with—tired now and worn thin from the wearisome toils Edgar had so long eschewed. Duncan's patience seemed to barely hang on as the precipice of Edgar's failing dignity grew slicker by the moment.

"Really, Edgar? You're still on this fucking self-righteous kick?" Duncan stepped forward now, his voice loud and rueful, yet his composure still unbroken.

"Self-righteous?" Edgar was in shock, "Really? How many times have all of you let me down? I know I've made the occasional mistake—hell, I'll be the first to admit I'm not perfect, Duncan. But that's supposed to be what friends are for, to listen and support each other until everything gets back on track.

"But that's just too much to ask from you, isn't it? Oh no, every time I came to you with anything, all I got was fucked over and left hanging. Guilt trips and judgment—way to have my fucking back!" Edgar paced angrily as he unleashed his tirade.

Duncan gaped, his mouth trembling visibly. He moved to speak, paused, closed his eyes and drew a long, deep breath. Opening his eyes, he finally continued in a slow, measured tone. "Let down? Fucked over? Come on, Edgar. You're a smart guy. I know that. How damn long are you going to go on blaming cruel, misplaced faith for destroying everything you touch before you step back and see the common fucking denominator?"

"Fuck you!" Edgar screeched, finding, in the end, he had nothing else left to say.

"Yeah, fuck you!" Jake lunged forward. His thick arm wound back, then shot out with a flash, catching Duncan in the jaw with a mighty crack.

Duncan hit the ground, blood pouring from his broken mouth and pooling on the cement, spreading over the congealed puddles from Edgar's lifeless corpse still hanging above—a silent sentinel to the misdeeds below.

Edgar flew into action. His outstretched knee took Jake in the ribs and sent the big man reeling. "What are you doing, you fucking idiot?" he yelled, shoving Jake again as he tried to regain his footing. Jake's candle fell to the ground, fizzling out in the mess of blood and dirt.

"Goddamn it!" Edgar screamed as Jake stared at him in consternation. "You're meant for one fucking thing Jake: to keep me entertained as I get my shit sorted. You clueless fuck! Stay out of things you can't understand!" Edgar pushed Jake again, hard, and watched with contempt as his sad, bewildered face disappeared into the all-consuming fog surrounding them.

Then he was gone.

Edgar stood alone beside Duncan, and the grey, steaming fog was their world. Behind them hung Edgar's macabre cadaver, and the church tower rose menacingly above all.

Rolling on the ground, Duncan cradled his shattered mouth with both hands. "I hope you're finally happy," said Edgar.

Duncan pulled himself up from the bloody ground, cringing as he stood. Blood painted his jaw like a satiated predator. "Happy?" he asked, his voice cracking as his mangled face quivered with rage. "Fuck you, Edgar. I've known you your whole life, and you've always gotten everything you ever wanted. If you're not happy with what you've got now, that's on you."

"You have no fucking idea what you're talking about," Edgar answered, his voice clad in steel.

Duncan shook his head, disgust and age making an ugly mask of his once handsome face. "Maybe you're right, Edgar. Maybe I really don't know you anymore. But I did once. So did you. And I promise you," he trembled with long-buried contempt as he spat his last venomous words, "if you don't figure out who you are and where you're going—and do it damn soon—then you've still got a long, lonely road ahead of you."

The alley was dark and hot, and the coppery scent of blood mingled with the sulfur stench of the fog.

Edgar stared through Duncan, wondering how things had ever gotten to this point. It didn't make sense. All his life, he'd been told that things would work out. But even Edgar's faith had reached its limit in the blood and turmoil of the alley of his death. With Duncan's pleading, wet eyes fixed on him and the church tower looming indignantly above, Edgar finally understood that he had only himself to blame.

"Go fuck yourself, Duncan," he said.

Duncan's shoulders slumped. Turning away, Edgar reached into his back pocket and lit up a smoke. Then he walked off into the hot, reeking fog towards the church tower—determined to confront the one person who still remained to him.

CHAPTER 10
THE BELLY OF THE BEAST

For as long as he could remember, Monday mornings for Edgar Vincent had been a humble exercise in recovery and redirection. On many such mornings he'd awoken and, upon determining to leave the debauchery of Saturday and suffering of Sunday behind him, Edgar would sit alone at his desk, get to work on his music, and focus on what lay ahead.

Mondays for Edgar had never been a thing to dread, as they weren't the usual return to commitment and drudgery so hated by more typical men. No, to Edgar, Mondays had always felt like great opportunities for personal growth.

In this context, he always felt he could be his truest self—and what a self that was! If asked to describe himself at any given time, Edgar might choose from a litany of wild stories and grand adjectives to capture the fine affair that was his life.

If asked what sort of lover he was, you could be certain Edgar would regale his inquisitor with outrageous and more-often-than-not vile tales of his nocturnal activities.

"'Nocturnal' indeed?" he might protest with a derisive sneer. Mornings, afternoons, evening walks—there was a story for every hour on the clock.

After that initial surge of bravado had passed, however, Edgar might feel further inclined to defend himself as a lover in the truest sense. If the mood struck him, he may go so far as to explain how he'd just never found the time to settle down. If especially inebriated, he might even tell you all about how the right one managed to slip right by him.

But none of that would be quite true.

It was true, certainly, that Edgar considered himself a great many things to a great many people. A friend? Edgar could talk for days about his unfailing loyalty and constant efforts to inspire his comrades to greater and more memorable deeds.

An artist? The stories might never stop! Edgar considered himself a pioneer of audio accompaniment. He could prattle on incessantly about his

141

achievements, and the depths of emotion he could unearth with a single note. Of course, he'd assure you, in the end, none of this held a candle to what was just around the corner.

Was Edgar a dutiful man? Just ask him! While he'd be the first to tell you he was a born rebel, he would also be the first—and quite likely the only—to tell you how tirelessly he worked for the betterment of those around him. "A genuine philanthropist," he'd claimed on one occasion, and on the occasion in question, the bartender who was his company wasn't inclined to disagree.

He'd been a loyal son, as he could elucidate with numerous examples.

He'd been an honest citizen, and he'd argue to the death that his selfless honesty and lack of ego made him a martyr for free thinkers the world over.

Yes, for any question and every doubt, Edgar had a handful of stories to demonstrate his uncanny devotion to truth and decency. He was, after all, a talented man, who yearned only to share his fun-loving outlook with the less enlightened refuse of humanity.

Or so he'd be happy to tell you, if circumstances provided.

But everyone has their stories, and everyone has to find their own truths.

In truth, Edgar was not the man he thought he was.

As he opened his tired eyes, he searched for clouds and arches.

There were none.

Where he might have expected enticing angels and eager friends, he found empty spaces. The roof above was high and flat, and morbid paintings covered the walls.

Sitting up slowly, he rubbed a patch of pebbles from where his cheek had rested in uneasy slumber. Then, knuckling his tired eyes, he gazed out over the scene awaiting him. Long, vacant rows of benches faced him expectantly.

His head swam as he turned it, and a brilliant white glow behind him threatened to run roughshod through the defensive squint of his eyelids. Looking around cautiously, he saw towering above him a humongous, illuminated cross. Golden spikes jutted menacingly out from its corners, and the bloody, beaten figure hanging upon it sent a self-conscious shiver along his throbbing spine.

Reaching blindly, he grasped a table covered in a pale purple cloth and pulled himself painfully to his feet. His innards roiled, and his universe spun; a hamster trapped by the momentum of its own unchecked ambition. Retching, he held the table desperately to avoid toppling over into a mess of his own sickness.

The air was thick and hot—laden with dizzying fragrances of burning candles and delicate incenses, which set off ancient alarms in Edgar's weary mind.

Fucking church. Edgar was incensed upon realizing where he was.

He took a careful step forward, and the floor groaned beneath him—a dreadful echo piercing the eerie silence of the church. A heavy golden chalice upon the table proved empty, as did several sparkling crystal decanters he checked along a lurching, uncertain stroll.

Even worse than I remembered, he lamented.

But memory is an impending landslide, and where one comes, others are sure to follow. They came in a rush, a torrent of regret and despair which—coupled with his lingering intoxication—sent Edgar stumbling against a wall draped in a tapestry intricately sewn with images of blood and whips, tears and torment.

Death. It came back to him all at once—the alley, the arguments, and the haunting realization that he was to blame for it all.

He'd been running from the facts. Running for longer than he cared to admit, yet running towards it all on the night he died. Edgar knew instinctually that he stood now beneath the great tower from the night before—the tower that had drawn him away from friends and comfort and meaning with the hollow promise of a chance to start anew.

Why the fuck did I come here? he wondered. But the answer held the coattails of the question, and Edgar's mind was a tempest of feeble excuses and farcical justifications. Compelled by some strange intuition, a glance to his right revealed a pair of thick wooden doors heralding his fate like personalized tombstones and empty grave plots.

With an indolent sigh, Edgar let his proud posture collapse as he realized the gravity of his predicament. He trembled under the weight of a splitting headache and fought waves of nausea with the hopeless resolve of a captain watching the water crest over the prow of his ship. He stood in a place more uncomfortable than any other he could imagine—and he was alone.

The necessity of the situation can hardly be denied. It's time to confess.

With tremulous steps and a pounding skull, Edgar walked over to the door on the right. His torn jacket sat heavy on his shoulders, still dripping with blood and clinging to his worn body in the unearthly heat.

The door rested slightly ajar, and he pulled it slowly open. This sent a chilling creak through the church, which rebounded back upon him—a mournful cry through a lonely canyon. With each passing second, Edgar sank deeper into the mires of his doubt.

Stepping inside and tugging the door fast behind him, an old, self-conscious dread welled up from years long past.

Darkness ruled within. Taking a seat on a tiny wooden bench, he rubbed the sweat from his brow as he took in the dismal scene. The room was cramped and seemed only to grow smaller with each panicked glance he cast this way and that. The walls were old and worn, and scratched deeply into them were the names of everyone Edgar had ever known.

This doesn't bode well, he admitted.

If the main room of the church had been hot, the confession booth was utterly intolerable. Each breath he drew caused him to choke and gasp as if his lungs were searing, and the bench grated his ass like rough straw and rusty razors.

Just in front of him was a small door designed to slide partly open, revealing a lattice screen through which the penitent could unburden himself. Edgar's skin crawled. His mouth was sandpaper, cutting and scraping at his tongue as he contemplated his next move.

Still, the suffocating heat raged above all else. Rising to a half-squat, he wiggled his shoulders and tugged on his sleeves. With an appreciative sigh, he let his tattered jacket plop down onto the bench. Settling back down upon it, he reached forward and knocked reluctantly on the delicate sliding door separating him from his confessor.

No voice came in answer, and the barrier remained in place.

Just as well, he reasoned, *no better company than self.*

"Hello?" he tried, his voice choked with dread. The routine was familiar to him—ingrained long ago in his young mind.

The practice was another story.

After a brief wait, Edgar gave a hesitant tug at the little sliding door. "Jesus Christ!" he screamed as it shattered into tiny shards, many embedding themselves into the soft flesh of his palm. Beyond was blackness—the deepest, most impenetrable void Edgar had ever seen. Whether it stretched on forever or ended immediately he couldn't tell, but sitting in its forefront was a sight that sent chills through his sweltering body. Resting on the cusp of nothing was a bottle of scotch wrapped in a dusty black tie.

He knew them immediately as the reserves formerly concealed in his office desk at home. *The BHI completion scotch.* The revelation churned his stomach and brought a burst of bile coursing up his throat. His muscles tensed and his adrenaline surged, preparing for fight or flight.

But Edgar had nothing left to fight for, and nowhere left to run.

Well, he reasoned with the intricate trickery of a child justifying his exposed indiscretions, *I did recently complete what is undoubtedly the greatest project I'll ever have…*

As a flash of fond—and moreover appalling—memories passed before his eyes, Edgar deemed that *Basic Human Indecency* would be as fitting a label for his life as it would have been for the eternally forsaken documentary. In that case, it only followed that the time had finally come to celebrate the great ambition that would now never reach fruition. With a churlish sneer, he brushed the tie aside and grabbed the bottle eagerly.

"Oh shit," he wailed, recoiling in pain as the bottle clattered to the hard wooden floor. The flesh of his right hand sizzled and peeled, and the scent of charred meat filled the cramped confines of the confessional.

"What the hell was that?" he demanded. The bottle rolled into the corner, waves of heat radiating up from it as Edgar held his hand and squinted through the pain. But the old tie still waited for him; cast aside, yet eternally patient. "First things first, I guess. Now's no time to buck tradition," he accepted with a grimace.

Trepidation filled his aching body as he took up the tie. It was filthy and faded—more grey than black now, and none of its original charm remained in the greasy and tattered rag it had become.

He remembered when he'd first worn it at his high-school graduation. His mother Rosa, his Nana Vasquez, even his father Eli had been there, smiling up at him in what Edgar could only assume had been a wild concoction of intrinsic pride and resounding relief that he'd actually managed to find his way through the tumultuous high school years. Edgar had stood defiantly on the edge of the stage, fingering the slick new tie as he gazed out on the world he would soon claim for his own.

It was the only tie he'd ever owned in his adult life, and it had seen him through university forums, graduations, job interviews, countless dates with "classy" ladies, and even a few funerals. However, it had long ago been relegated to the desk drawer, resurrected only to celebrate the completion of whatever major project he found himself scoring. When those increasingly rare moments came, Edgar was uncharacteristically rigid about tradition: first, he would fasten the sad old tie around his neck, then he'd crack open the bottle of scotch. Finally, relaxing in quiet repose, he would drink with a proud smile as he listened to his newly finished composition.

One last hurrah, old boy, he thought and secured the tie lazily around his sweat-soaked neck. With that out of the way, Edgar looked down at the scotch. The visible heat pulsing up had dissipated into the somewhat less intense burning of the air all about. With one careful touch, then another, Edgar concluded the bottle was safe at last. With the tie in its place, the scotch's time had come.

Taking it up delicately, he cracked it open with little fanfare but much relish. The black metal lid clattered to the floor as the warm glass rim met his lips. His nostrils thrilled, and the sharp, burning liquid soothed his throat. He helped himself to a long swallow, chasing away the lingering ghosts of the night before.

That's more like it, he acquiesced with a relieved smile.

"Hello?" he called again, to no avail. "It's been, well…" Edgar had to consider here, crunching numbers in his aching skull before concluding it was a fruitless endeavour. "Well, it's been a while since I last confessed."

Still, no answer came.

Edgar continued, surprising even himself with his single-minded determination. "I don't really remember how all this is supposed to go," he lied, "but I suppose it's time to touch base—to settle accounts, as they say."

Edgar was stalling.

Amongst all the indescribably obscene atrocities for which Edgar was entirely in need of confessing, he found himself at an impasse—namely, where to begin.

Tipping the fresh bottle high into the air, Edgar savoured the familiar burn. The Hall of Memories—its sights and revelations played out before him as he sat in contemplative silence. He recalled the earliest details of his childhood in the heavy Sunday air, and the brutal revelations of the alley the night before flashed like perverted pantomimes across the frail wooden walls of the confessional.

"I was trying to remember how many days I've been here," he started, "but it's all blurred together. Not like that's some kind of epiphany—it's always been that way.

"I've been wasting my time here, squandering an amazing opportunity. I know that, but facing the truth is never an easy thing to do.

"It's like Duncan said, I've been running my entire life. One day after another, each one carrying some excuse not to act. I've treated time like it was meaningless—some unlimited resource to be burned away with no care or thought. It was inevitable that I eventually ran out."

He took another swallow of scotch, then one more to force down the nervous lump welling up in his throat. Finally, he pushed on. "I grew up feeling like I was guaranteed so much—as if fantastic opportunities beyond count lay just over the horizon.

"But my generation never had any great calling. I was taught in broad strokes. I've always felt ready to defend my love or to support my children. If cornered in an alley or faced with dire straits in a foreign land, I'm certain I'd have what it takes.

"But I haven't. I've been faced instead with great stretches of boredom, and my sole enemy has been the treacherous mix of tedium and convenience. For that, I've proven less of a man than I'd hoped.

"Looking back now, I realize all the things I've missed out on—things I always thought would just happen. Having my own family, that's a big one. I took it for granted that it would come about eventually—that one day when I least expected it some ideal vixen would steal my heart and set everything right. It was in the back of my mind every night I went out, and with the first shot at each bar, I'd scan the room wondering if she was there, hiding somewhere in the shadows, waiting for her moment to shine.

"But one shot leads to another, and distraction always shone the brighter.

"I wanted to achieve the sort of artistic success I felt I deserved. Ever since Duncan and I were young, that was the plan. 'Rule the world', we'd always say." Edgar chuckled distantly, but his face was carved from stone. "BHI was supposed to do that. It really was the project I'd been waiting for. But I couldn't complete it. It sat for so long with just a few sections to finish. I know the director pretty much gave up on it, but not me. I never stopped believing I'd finish it, and then everything would be OK. I can't say for sure why I didn't. It's just that one thing would come up, then another.

"I guess that with so many strange stories and amusing encounters always going on, I failed to realize that's all I was doing: going on, day after day.

"Now it's all over, and when I look back on my life the distractions just blur together; one long hazy Sunday, with nothing to show for all the wasted time but a sense of weariness I just can't shake."

Edgar was exhausted.

"I know I was an asshole. It's pretty hard to deny from this vantage point. Still, I think I did some things right. I was headed in the right direction at least, even if the progress was slow."

Taking a long swill from his bottle, the warmth of the liquor combined with the sweltering confessional, creating an inferno inside him. He sat silently for a long while, sifting through the wreckage to filter out the few decent times in his life.

"I can't say exactly what I wanted to hear from Bev. In fact, I honestly can't imagine," he started, stealing another chug of whiskey as he wondered if the existential nature of his dilemma merited an explanation to the absent confessor.

No, fuck that, he decided.

"I realize it's strange that she's still in my thoughts. At least that's what many a woman has told me since. I don't know what it is, exactly. That memory just holds me fixated for reasons I could never quite articulate. What is it about her that made no other woman worthy?"

Edgar considered this for a moment, but nothing came to him besides a dirty joke.

"Maybe it's a product of the time. Or maybe it's just the easiest time to look back on," he speculated. "I suppose I was at my very best back then, starting out with a head full of promise. Whatever the reason, I was never a better man than I was with Bev."

Reflecting for a second on the countless mistakes and lies, the silence of the confessional was a terrible burden. *Even with Bev, I was never an especially good man,* he accepted with a defeated sigh.

Clenching his eyelids to force back the pounding in his skull, Edgar watched the sordid history of his love life play through his mind's eye. Women desperate for connection pleaded with him. Their wet and sparkling eyes were inevitably met with only a cold gaze and flippant joke.

The cramped wooden bench was rough even through his jacket, catching and pulling with each small movement, and on the walls were sharp knobs and points waiting to catch an errant arm. From deep within the sable void before him, visions of the angels danced: Tyra with her red lips and sensuous smile, Tiffany's youthful exuberance and empty head. He witnessed Leslie's vice-fuelled glee and recalled the comforting insights of Chanel's passionate intellect. Jasmine's classy curves bounced in her expensive silks. All were overplayed and utterly trite—the sorts of twisted caricatures to which Edgar could so easily boil any woman down at a glance.

What kind of man can conjure up any woman he wants, and end up hating the result? He shuddered and took a hard swallow from his bottle, striving to dodge the impending answer.

It had always been the same—whenever things got too serious, Edgar would bail. He'd run away like a scared child, making cynical jokes to his friends while secretly reminiscing about easier times, as if they excused his present behaviour.

"It's unfair, but I guess Bev was the measuring rod I used ever since.

"I hope," he finished sadly, "I haven't derailed too many other great stories as I've struggled to glorify my own."

Edgar was afraid.

Passing a hand over his brow, he sighed under the hot blanket of the confessional's interior. The tie bit like a viper into the bare flesh of his neck. His forehead was damp with sweat. He was weak with dehydration, yet the feeling of a cigarette rubbing against his hand from behind his ear painted an eager grin across his handsome but worn face.

Serendipity, he thought. Sparking it to life, he took a long drag and groaned with relief. A quick swallow of whiskey to wash down the stale flavour lingering in his mouth, and Edgar was in…

Well, still one shy of the Trinity, he joked. But female company was not a priority for Edgar just now.

"I was always so focused on myself," he continued, staring ahead absently as he puffed on his smoke and sipped from his bottle. Part of him was beginning to feel rather proud of his newfound clairvoyance and personal insight, but the remainder understood that pride served only to flip the process back onto himself. So he let it slide and forged on determinedly.

"And not just with women, I realize that now. I was a constant letdown to my friends as well." The memories of the night before were hazy at best, yet Edgar didn't need a vivid recollection to know he'd treated his friends like complete shit.

Just a rudimentary knowledge of history.

"Alex and Emeric, Jake and Duncan. They all did so much for me in my life.

"What would I have been without Alex's subtle encouragements to find my own direction? I had the opportunity to finally reconnect with him after all these years, and I didn't do a damn thing different.

"And Emeric was just so fucking good-natured." Edgar couldn't help but laugh to himself, sending a long trail of smoke snaking from his mouth to twirl about in the steamy air around him. "To be honest, I don't even know why he hung out with me. I certainly did nothing to help him along the way. I treated him like a child and a coward, but he knew exactly where he was going and got there in spite of my teasing.

"Jake is a different story, mind you." Edgar was caught up in his own momentum now and no longer stopped to consider his confessor's absence.

It wasn't really the point.

"That dolt would do anything for me, but I just used him for an ear—

an excuse to go out and get hammered without running the risk of being that lonely drunk at the bar. And I've got to give it to the guy, he served his purpose well.

"I hope I get the chance to thank the dumb bastard." Edgar laughed, and took another pull from his bottle.

"And of course there's Duncan, my oldest friend. I have memories of Duncan that date back earlier than memories of my immediate family. To be honest, he's probably been the most consistent factor in my life. Without fail, he believed in me through it all. He never lost sight of my potential, even when I was a blazing contradiction to everything he thought of me.

"But I only paid him back with spite and scorn, acting like he didn't understand me." Edgar twirled the cigarette between his fingers, lazily flicking the tip onto the floor and watching the blazing embers simmer out into dull ash.

"I hope I'll get to make it up to them," he mused. But wondering exactly how much control he still had over his afterlife caused his head to spin, and gazing again at his surroundings made an angry sea of his stomach. "They were the first familiar people I saw here, yet I went straight back into my old habits despite their warnings."

Edgar shook his head, ignoring the protests of his aching skull as his hands clenched into fists of stone. The burn on his right hand sent painful sirens screeching through his mind, but ultimately went ignored. "Dammit, I've always been this way. Pushing away the important things—avoiding what matters for fear that it might vanish on closer inspection.

"This self-destructive urge has been in me as long as I can remember. I can't say why, but it seems to be one of the few things that followed along into this realm—an intrinsic part of me I just can't shake.

"I did it with Bev, I did it with BHI, and I did it with my friends in life. Then I got up here, got a fresh start, and I fucking did it all over again.

"If nothing's changed, and I'm stuck here forever, then what's the point? My afterlife is pointless!" Slamming his fist against the rickety wood-paneled wall sent a thunder crack through the confessional, and Edgar cowered in his seat.

Then, collecting his composure, he realized sadly the lie of his previous declaration.

No, he corrected himself, *my life was pointless.*

A hit of his bottle settled his beating heart, and with a great force of will, he stiffened his upper lip before continuing. "But at least I know that now. I know where I fell short. There's a great deal I wish I could change, but that's beyond me now." Edgar ran his dry tongue over cracking lips.

"I tried to be decent, even if I failed. But if I ever have the chance again, I know I'd set it right. No more mistakes. Not now. I never wanted to hurt anyone; I wanted to be the man they all deserved. I definitely failed, but still, I did try."

Edgar was a liar.

"I remember," he pushed on, unsure if the honest reflection or the bottle in his hand deserved the credit for his slowly increasing enthusiasm. "I was so certain things would work out. It's what I was always told, and for a long time, it seemed true enough. Little mistakes don't amount to much for a young man, but they begin to stack up with the years.

"Under the assumption that things will always be fine, it's easy to ignore the casualties on the endless road to satisfaction."

Edgar took another swig from the whiskey bottle before returning it to his lap. "I barely knew my father, but my mother was a constant source of comfort. Still, it was my grandmother who made the biggest impression. She always assured me that God had a special purpose for me, and I just needed to have faith that it may be fulfilled. It's what I was taught from a young age, and I still have trouble accepting that it wasn't really true."

He paused a moment, taking a slow pull from his cigarette as he chuckled to himself, half-amused at the situation's irony, half-disappointed by his own naïve hope that some assurance might still come.

"We sang songs, recited prayers," he finally went on. "I was told constantly that a pure heart was what really counted. But that's the way with religions— they're for the living.

"Maybe it's all bullshit. Maybe we don't really need it. Then again maybe we're just such stupid, mindless creatures; that without some clear and irrefutable rules to follow, we're doomed to go mad.

"Or maybe that's just me…it doesn't matter anyway."

Mold was forming on the crusts of Edgar's motivation, and he shook his head hard to chase out his growing sense of unease. "I've made my choices, and I guess this is me accounting for them now. I want to be good; I want to make people happy. To those ends at least, I suppose my family's teachings were a success. There are certainly people who strive for less.

"Still, a good heart has served me exceptionally poorly when everything else is so fucking rotten. It takes more than faith and ignorance to navigate through life, and a blind eye serves only the vultures."

It struck him as funny how the existential nature of his dilemma no longer seemed especially strange. His cigarette was making a brave last stand, and a quick hit of scotch told him his bottle wasn't doing much better.

"I certainly maintained at least a vague idea of where I wanted to go. But I was always content, and I always felt safe. Maybe that's what kept me from making significant changes in my life. It just never occurred to me to trust in anything but time to get me there. I considered it part of my charm—the flippancy and avoidance—they just made my inevitable success that much more impressive.

"I wish I'd started earlier, but that's the power of hindsight—especially in a place like this. I had what it takes; I don't think anyone would deny that. Maybe if I'd had better inspirations, or if I hadn't placed my faith in fatalism and taken personal responsibility instead, things would have worked out better. Who can say?

"Perhaps that's the real lesson beneath blind faith, and I've just learned it a bit too late."

Edgar was a phony.

He sighed, feeling utterly naked in the dim, hot silence of the booth. The edges of the bench tore at his tired legs—straight razors forming the walls of a sadistic holding cell. In front of him, the inky void twisted and morphed before his eyes, etching images of suffering and torment into his worn-out mind.

The light in the confessional was dim, but what little there was appeared to flicker—the entire enclosure lit as if by roaring fires sufficient to account for its overwhelming heat. Edgar's head still throbbed, and his squeamish guts roiled with the potent cocktail of Sunday sickness and candid introspection.

"I know," he began again, hesitating just long enough to take a quick swill from his bottle. He coughed and sputtered as the noxious flavour hit his tongue, then continued. "I always knew things needed to change. It was simply a matter of when. It felt like I had a lifetime ahead of me—time to re-evaluate and plan—but more importantly, time to stay lost in the comfort just a little while longer.

"I guess it keeps coming back to time. Life must always do that when it begins to grow short. Wish I had more, but wasted what I had…it's all the same shit.

"I never intended to squander my opportunities, not consciously at least. I always had an escape plan, ready to go into effect on any given tomorrow. But that never comes. Each day is written off before it begins: one more day of freedom or one final day of recovery. One or the other, then the cycle continues back around. But it's never too late…"

…*until it is.*

The space remained silent, and peering at the jet-black hole to the other side, he let his bottle rest in his lap. The room looked strange, blurred and distorted as if a thin veil of smoke hung between Edgar's eyes and his reality. "Despite how satisfied I felt with where I was, I'd never have said it was where I wanted to end up. It started as a pit stop of sorts, but the road was so easy, and I guess the distractions eventually overtook the destination.

"Even up here, it somehow seemed like I'd have plenty of time to get around to what mattered. I knew I had to do the decent things and have the tough conversations, but there were other things to do as well. I've never in my life been an unhappy man; it's just that a swallow of whiskey or the touch of a woman has always promised to make me even happier."

Edgar was lost.

He took a deep drag from the cigarette hanging limply in his mouth. Holding his breath, his head rolled and the room wheeled about madly. Exhaling slowly, he watched the smoke coil around like dragon's breath, wreathing his monastic trappings in its reeking haze.

"Who the hell was I? What did I think made me so different?" Edgar asked with a cynical laugh. Only silence met his question, but he smiled, easing back on the hard wooden bench and letting his mass slide down the rough backrest. He was growing strangely comfortable with the quiet and wondered if that was all he'd ever needed—a chance to hear himself: unjustified, unrestrained. The booth was free of judgment, and that only made its inevitable verdict all the more profound.

"I used to think of myself as a rebel. I don't remember when it started, but my path always went the other way—cutting through the undergrowth of bullshit to the hidden temples of truth. But the irony of being a man defined by his road to redemption is that any effort to change your circumstances makes a lie of your image. So I never stopped to question it. There never even seemed to be any real need—as if my every distant intention was somehow more significant, simply by virtue of it being my own.

"But I guess it didn't work out that way. I blazed my own trails, no doubt. But where have I ended up? I'm an adversary to the handful of friends I have, and a predator to the few remaining women who don't already know better.

"I always thought I was born to be one of a kind," Edgar spoke into the ether, "I just never bothered to consider exactly what kind that was."

The bench caught and tore at the battered jacket beneath him with each small shift, and a slow pounding began to punch through the quiet air. The rumbling dirge welled up to suffocate the peaceful calm, a rising Gregorian chant which brought Edgar a terrible sense of finality.

"It's a funny line to walk—being pulled between the joys and regrets both so inherent in a life well-lived. It was a life of calamity no doubt, but at least I've got my stories. That's one thing I'm certain of; despite all the heinous mistakes I've made, I know I created some decent memories for those poor bastards I left behind.

"I just hope they remember them—long after they've forgotten all the rest."

Another drag, and another swig, yet the squirming feeling in Edgar's stomach would not subside. The smoke burned his eyes, and he knuckled them roughly. He dripped with sweat, and his raw throat protested his continued soliloquy.

"I remember one time, at the end of second year." Edgar grinned with the recollection. It had been a long while since he'd stopped to reflect in any sincere way. "Exams were nearly over, and I knew that in a week the five of us would go our separate ways for the summer. Alex would go to his hometown to do whatever it was Alex did for money, and Duncan would find some highbrow volunteer position to pad his résumé. Emeric would end up burying his face in independent studies for the summer, and I'd be left to carry on the legacy with Jake in their absence.

"There were still a few exams left, as I was reminded so many times, but I thought we needed a special little something to commemorate the end of the year. A celebration of sorts—just for the inner circle."

The air was dry and hot, and every word pained Edgar. Still, he continued, more calm and content than he'd felt in years. "I'd managed to steal most of their notes earlier in the week, and phoned each of them with tailor-made reasons to meet me in the old park by the residence buildings.

"I told Duncan I had big news. He probed for a while but finally acquiesced. Lucky thing, since I'd never planned his excuse beyond that. I just told him I needed him there, and never doubted he'd come.

"I told Jake I'd found a keg; that one was simple. For Alex, I said I'd met some local players who had some interesting things to show him—he didn't even ask any questions, only said he was on his way.

"Emeric was a bit more difficult, I really had to put on a show for him by that point. In the end though, I boiled it down by saying I needed his help, and sure enough, he showed up with the others.

"They were a bit pissed when they realized it was a ruse, and even more so when they found their missing notes in the big pit I'd dug. Well, Duncan and Emmy were. Alex didn't really care, and Jake didn't have any notes to contribute anyway.

"But when I lit the pile up and pulled out the fireworks and booze, they all came around." Edgar's voice strove against him, and came in staccato bursts between brief periods of silence. "We all stood there by the blazing notes, drinking and watching the fireworks.

"Alex said it was beautiful.

"Jake gave an emphatic 'Hell's yeah!'

"Even Emmy had to admit he was impressed.

"And Duncan, he just looked over with a big grin, shaking his head as his face lit up in the reds and greens and yellows of the fireworks exploding high above.

"That was a pretty great night," Edgar finished, taking a quick nip of whiskey to steady his excited heart. "If more of my time down there could have been like that, I'd be a lot happier being here."

But times had seldom gone so well for Edgar. His selfish focus had always conspired to turn circumstances against him, and his blind passion consistently prevented him from learning any legitimate lessons.

"Looking back, the world was never really the caring place I was raised to expect. It didn't eagerly await my contributions, or patiently accept my missteps.

"But it wasn't a cold, manipulative series of events conspiring against me either, even though I often treated it as such. In truth, I guess the world just didn't care. One way or another, it went on spinning in oblivious apathy, unmoved by any of my hopeless failings; asking nothing, expecting nothing." Edgar sighed, easing into his epiphany like a child into an icy bath.

That was the secret, the ultimate truth of Edgar Vincent, which had eluded him for so long: it was all up to him.

"So here I am, in Hell. It's not what I was led to imagine. There's no fire, no whips." Edgar ran his burned hand down the faded length of his old tie. "It's just…me."

Without faith…

"A man is only what he does with his life," Edgar finished the thought.

"I spent so much time trying to create stories to look back on, yet I managed to get myself killed before I had the chance to appreciate them.

I know I made my share of mistakes—more than my share if we're being honest—but still..." Words finally failed Edgar, and with one last puff, he snuffed out his cigarette on the dusty floor of the confessional.

Without his stories, Edgar was nothing.

Shaking his head, Edgar knew he still had a long way to go.

And no shortage of time to get there, he assured himself with a coy grin.

Standing, he pulled on his torn and bloody jacket despite the heat. It was dirty and worn—familiar and comfortable. With a crack of his knuckles, he reached up and tugged the collar tight against his neck, causing the old tie to tear savagely at his skin. Straightening his back despite the pain, he struggled to resume the confident posture that had always come so naturally.

Opening the door to his left, the inky fog pressed menacingly against his exit. He shuddered. The dead air without did nothing to quench the smouldering furnace within. Reaching into his back pocket, Edgar pulled out his packet of smokes. His fingers fumbled around in the void of the case, twisting and searching for a comfort that was beyond him now. Finally, he peered in to find it empty.

"Fuck."

Letting the spent pack drop to the floor with an impotent flop, he reached up to massage his throbbing temples. Then, clutching his whiskey bottle tightly in his burnt right hand, Edgar stepped out into the darkening fog of what was to come.

Sunday had arrived. Still, Monday felt a long way off.